PANDEI

JEAN HARVEY

APS PUBLICATIONS

Pandemic

Copyright ©2018 APS Publications

Proof reading by tayladalziel@hotmail.co.uk

APS Publications,

4 Oakleigh Road, Stourbridge, West Midlands, DY8 2JX

www.andrewsparke.com

1

The barefoot young woman carefully picked her way through the debris. Even though her dirty hair was tangled, and her face and clothes were smeared with soot, there was no doubt that she was beautiful. She was carrying a wooden bowl containing soup for the old lady, and as she neared the sleeping woman, she gently called out her name so as not to alarm her.

"Annie," she called again, this time a little louder.

The woman stirred. She looked up through blurry pale blue eyes at the silhouette leaning over her.

"I've brought you some soup," said the girl. "Could you eat some if I help you?"

"I'll try." Annie struggled to pull herself up. "Who are you?"

"I'm Mary."

The young woman spooned the warm soup into Annie's mouth but after two mouthfuls Annie flopped back exhausted onto her sheepskin bed. "Sorry. I can't manage any more."

"Just try to sleep. You've had quite a shock." Mary gently covered the old woman with another sheepskin to keep her warm. When she knelt over Annie to make sure she was comfortable, their eyes met. The old eyes were a misty blue and very tired. The young eyes were bright, the most amazing hazel colour, outlined in black.

Annie tried hard to hold the young one's gaze as she struggled to remember where she had seen eyes like those before, but she couldn't do so. As she desperately tried to recall what had happened, the struggle became too much. She was so weary that she couldn't think. Her heavy eyelids closed and soon she was fast asleep.

Mary decided it would be alright to leave her sleeping for a time whilst she went down to the river to wash both herself and her dirty, soot-covered clothes.

Annie dreamed of her Mum, Doreen, and the exciting bedtime stories she'd told her and her sister, Barbara. Their Mum held them enraptured with her storytelling, always stopping at an exciting part to say, "Off to bed now." Then next night when they eagerly awaited the continuation of the story, Mum would rub her chin, and say, "Now, where was I?" The two girls always knew exactly where the story had finished the previous night. Years later their Mum told them that she'd had no idea where the story had reached because she made it up as she went along.

Annie smiled in her dreams.

"You should write a book Mum," Annie used to say.

"Not educated enough," her Mum would always reply.

In her younger days Mum had had the most beautiful copper coloured hair and eyes. As she got older her hair became streaked with white. Nothing gave her greater pleasure than to huddle on the settee, hugging her girls, letting them know she loved them. She never complained no matter how much pain she was in, and Annie remembered her Mum's last words just before she died from the cancer. She was in hospital at the end and Annie was about to release her hand, and step away from her bedside, when she opened her eyes, and, gripping Annie's hand tightly, said croakily, "You know that I've always loved you, don't you?" With that, she closed her eyes and she was gone. Annie, with tears streaming down her face, had to move aside for the nurse. Those few words stayed with Annie for the rest of her life, and whenever she thought about it, goose-bumps ran down her spine, and tears seeped into her eyes.

Annie stirred in her sleep and wiped away the tears with the back of her hand.

Before long, Dad came into her dreams. Unlike Mum, he was very strict. He was always smartly dressed, never going out without a shave, even to work in the mine. He'd put on a clean shirt and tie every night after work if he was going out. He had old corduroy trousers and a few shirts with frayed collars he wore for working in the garden. She seldom remembered him ever laughing with them, but he was always the rock of the family if ever anything was going wrong. He was also the one to whom all their neighbours and workmates turned to for help with any problem. He knew who to contact if someone had tried to *rip you off*, as he called it, or if your wages were not correct – unlike most of the others, he wasn't afraid to approach the Management in those days.

He took good care of the family finances, and they always seemed to have enough while others struggled. Annie remembered Dad joining the Union. Everyone did but he always wanted to make a difference, and was picked to become a delegate, attending meetings to help negotiate better deals for the men, not just for more money but for better safety equipment because working in the mines was very dangerous.

People were always coming to their house to see if *Our Jack* could help them out with this or that, especially after he was elected onto the Council. Doreen never seemed to mind spending hours on her own. She just got on with things, and her daughters never heard her complain about Dad being off on some business or other. Dad was well-respected and handsome with very dark wavy hair held down with a slick of Brylcreem. He must have been about six feet tall and very muscular from working at the coalface. Doreen told her girls it had been his eyes which attracted her in the first place – they were the brightest blue she had ever seen, reminding her of the sky on a hot summer day.

Dad was always on the trail of something to help his constituents and never seemed to tire. He would come home from work, having started at six in the morning, lie on the settee for ten to fifteen minutes and then, refreshed, he'd wash and change before eating his evening meal and heading out for meetings, or to see constituents. He loved the role of councillor and didn't retire from it until he was eighty-five.

One day, Barbara went to visit him as she did every morning. She found him sitting in his favourite chair with a smile on his face, a peaceful passing in every respect. Barbara and Annie had assumed his funeral would be a quiet one like their Mum's years before. They didn't foresee all of the people he'd helped turning up to pay their respects. The church was packed. People congregated outside so the vicar opened the doors to let them hear the service. Afterwards, the two women were overwhelmed by people shaking their hands and telling them what a grand chap *Old Jack* had been. The sisters recognised hardly any of them but were touched by the sentiments they expressed.

Years before, Dad had told them that under no circumstances were they to make a fuss when he died. He used to say that they could bury him in the back garden for all he was bothered. He would not have bargained for this turnout. The cancer research collection box near the church door contained over £2,000 when it was counted, to their dumb-founded amazement.

Annie smiled in her sleep, nestling in the comforting memories of her parents. Snuggling down into the warmth of her sheepskin covers, she drifted off to when she was a child.

One thing which had always been talked about was the time when Annie, at about three years old, was found sitting in a field with a bull. In her sleep, Annie grinned. She couldn't actually remember the event, but it had been talked about so often that it had become very real to her.

This is how the story went – Mum had recycled an old dark-red coat into a siren suit. Such suits had a hood and long sleeves and legs with buttons fastening up the front so that a child could easily be slipped into one to keep warm when making the urgent journey to the air raid shelter after the sirens went off during the war.

Barbara, who was about eight years old, took Annie and the other children to play in one of the farmer's fields. They were always freer to roam in those days. They were all sitting, happily making daisy chains, when a bull, previously unnoticed, started across from the other side of the field. A cry went up from one of the children. Barbara yelled for the others to run for the safety of the gate and they all did, except for Annie who was contentedly joining up daisies, blissfully unaware of the danger. He came closer and closer as she sat there warm and cosy in her new red siren suit until he stood right over her. She looked up but was too young to see any need to react and continued playing with the flowers.

Barbara ran as fast as she could to fetch Mum, who raced to the field. All she could see was the bull towering over her youngest child. She was too afraid to go into the field so the only thing she could do was run for the farmer. The farmhouse fortunately wasn't far and Mr Evans jumped onto his tractor with Mum perched on the mudguard as he sped down the track. He walked into the field with a long rod with a hook at the end of it calling out "Walter," as he neared the huge bull standing over the little girl. Neither moved a muscle as the farmer put the hook into the ring on the bull's nose to lead him away. Immediately Mum ran and scooped Annie up to carry her to safety but Mr Evans was smiling as he came over to where Doreen was holding the child in her arms.

"Sorry for the scare, but Old Walter is the gentlest of creatures. He wouldn't harm a fly. Did you see how he was protecting our Annie? I wouldn't have put him in the field if he was dangerous." He patted Mum's shoulder in reassurance but she just scowled.

Mr Evans always called her *Our Annie*. Every day he used to bring milk in a big churn and ladle out the amount Mum wanted into her jug when Annie was a baby, because she would not drink formula. The milk was from a cow called Daisy. All his cows had names and this kind man had a soft spot for little Annie.

Annie's thoughts turned to the house she had lived in as a child. The kitchen was just large enough for a table and four chairs, and when not in use for meals was pushed close to the wall. It was scrubbed clean, like a butcher's block, so her Mum could roll out pastry or knead dough for bread. A tiny room, separated from the kitchen by a wooden wall, housed a bath. The taps were big and bulbous and not attached to the bath, but to thick lead pipes fastened to the wall. Another door from the kitchen opened to a small square hallway with the front door and the stairs leading up to two bedrooms. The third door out of the kitchen led into a room containing a settee and two matching armchairs all with wide arms. This room opened in turn into a long, narrow garden and, as the last house in the row, it had a stone wall on one side which formed the back of the big house, which used to be the farmhouse. Before the garden proper, there was a yard area with a toilet and coalhouse. When coal was delivered it was tipped onto the street and Dad used his wheelbarrow to cart it down the side of the house and then shovelled it into the coalhouse.

At the bottom of the garden was a fence running in both directions as far as the eye could see. Beyond this fence was a grass-covered bank sloping down to the railway. At the bottom of the street was a place for crossing the lines to get to the Park. Wooden sleepers were in place between the railway lines forming a so-called level crossing.

Sometimes boys would put their ear onto the metal line to feel the vibration of an approaching train. If anyone had a penny they would put it on the line and run to clamber on the park fence and wave to the train as it whizzed past. As soon as it had gone by the lads would be off the fence to quickly retrieve the flattened penny.

On the Park was a cricket ground. Woe betide you if the park keeper saw you put a foot on it. There was a huge bandstand which was used by brass bands every weekend. In front of this was a cobblestone area where chairs would be put out so that people could sit down and listen to the band. Not far away, surrounded by a low, neatly trimmed privet hedge was an oblong paddling pool, always full of children splashing about when the weather was hot, and mothers sitting around it on blankets yelling at the bigger kids to mind the toddlers. Beyond that was a pitch-and-putt golf course. Not very big, but lots of fun. You could hire a golf club from a grumpy old man in a hut at the side of the bandstand. You got your money back when you returned the club.

The play area was always full of children. There was a *Mountain Slide* for bigger kids – an adult could not reach up to the top of the slide – and sometimes there could be fifteen children or more racing to the steps to climb up and then jumping off as quickly as possible at the bottom so the one behind didn't kick them. Then they'd race back to the steps and do it all again. They called it *Keeping the Kettle Boiling*. The game usually ended when some kid failed to move from the bottom quickly enough and was kicked by the next one who then couldn't get out of the way of the next one, stopping the flow completely.

The other favourite was *The Bobbies Helmet*, a big structure from which steel rods opened out like a big skirt and at the bottom, about a yard from the floor, it had a circle of wooden seats. The bigger children would sit and use their feet to get the whole thing moving round really fast and the smaller ones would hold on very tight, dreading what would happen if they fell off. Usually it was the boys in charge and the girls their age stopping them. This caused the children to run off, trying to get to the swings or roundabout before anyone else. Funny thing – children always seem to run everywhere.

Annie was racing along with them but suddenly she was wide awake.

2

With a great deal of effort, Annie struggled to sit up and look around her. She was very confused. One moment she was in the comfort of childhood memories, and then suddenly nothing was familiar.

Mary ran across to her as quickly as she could negotiate the rubble. She was still barefoot but now her long hair was flying out behind her, a clean blonde mass glistening in the bright sunshine. Her face and clothes were also clean and fresh.

Annie thought she recognised the girl. "Sharon?" she said, her dry throat croaking out the name.

Gently, Mary hugged her. "Sharon was my Great-Grandmother. I must look like her."

Before Annie could ponder that, Mary was carefully, but firmly, helping Annie to her feet. "Come on Annie. We're going to let you have a wash and some food and then we can tell you everything that's happened."

It was a struggle for Annie to walk. Her tired old bones creaked and groaned but she felt safe leaning on Mary's young and strong arm. They made their way over to a group of others who all seemed about the same age. They greeted her smiles. One of the girls held out a bowl of warm water to her.

"Can I go to the toilet first?" asked Annie.

"Course you can," said Mary. "Do you want me to help you?"

"Would you think me a terrible nuisance? I don't know where it is." Annie felt bemused by the whole situation. The others laughed but

Mary glared at them, shaking her head as she helped Annie to her feet again.

When Annie and Mary came back the others were all sitting cross-legged in a circle on the ground. Mary helped Annie to a wooden chair in the middle and the girl with the bowl of water proffered it again to Annie who dipped her fingers carefully and scooped water over her face, the girls scrutinising her every move. Annie was then handed a towel of sorts, old and very worn, more like a rag than anything else.

"My name's Emma." The girl was small and had long light brown hair plaited down each side of her face which somehow made her look even younger than her sixteen or so years. She had a ready smile showing gleaming white teeth.

"Thank you, 'Em...Emma," Annie stuttered, giving her back the towel without showing any sign of recognition.

Another girl came with a wooden bowl containing soup. Like Emma, she had long hair but thick and black, worn plaited down her back with some kind of vine holding it in place. "Would you like me to hold the bowl for you while you eat?" she asked, and again, Annie nodded. "I'm Lois," the youngster giggled as she handed Annie a spoon. She couldn't understand how Annie didn't know who she was. She held the bowl close enough so Annie could spoon the food into her mouth. Lois wasn't thin like the others but a little chubby which somehow reminded Annie of herself at that age, and how she and her friends had giggled at everything. For a second Annie thought she remembered something significant, but it was just a fleeting moment, gone as quickly as it had come into her mind.

"This is my twin brother, Liam," Lois turned and pointed him out. The resemblance was obvious. They both had the same olive complexion, very dark brown eyes, and black hair, although Liam's was curly and cut close to his head.

He was just as cheerful as his sister. "Hi Annie," he said, grinning at her, showing pearly white teeth. All that the old woman could do was nod to him. It was all so confusing for her as she could not remember any of them.

Mary intervened quickly. She could see that Annie was getting distressed, so she introduced Adam, Craig and Josh, who just nodded and waved in Annie's direction.

Adam had cut his platinum blonde hair with a sharp knife. Annie noticed his feet and hands and his bright sky-blue eyes twinkling for her. It was beyond her to remember whom she had known with equally large hands and feet. Loss of memory was so harrying and it showed on her face as Mary watched her closely.

Craig had dark red hair and freckles. Mary had to continuously give him balm to rub into his skin to stop it burning in the endless sunshine. He was much heavier in build than the rest of the youngsters, perhaps because his job involved less physical activity. He was their beekeeper. Josh had straw coloured hair and pale blue eyes and was tall by comparison. He seemed full of enthusiasm, eager and excited with everything.

After several mouthfuls of the delicious soup, Annie had eaten enough, and Lois stepped forward – again giggling – to take away the bowl and spoon. Then, Annie pointed to each of them in turn, trying to recall each of their names. Although they were all around sixteen years old, they were still children to Annie. When she could not match names to faces she became agitated and upset. She knew that she must know them all but had no previous recollection of any of them.

"That's enough for now," stated Mary. "Everything will come back to you, but we have to get you back to lie down and rest." Without further ado, she carefully steered Annie back to her resting place. Helping her onto the sheepskin bed she said, "Rest now, Annie. It's all been such a shock." Annie lay down, obediently.

Once Mary left her, Annie thought to herself: *What's been a shock? Is it something to do with the reason why I can't remember anything? Or is it so horrible, my brain's shut everything out?* She found her thoughts drifting again into what she could remember. Her past life.

3

The name Sharon popped into Annie's mind. *Sharon; my best friend Sharon. This is where it all began, but where was Sharon? Surely, she'd know what to do.* Annie remembered that Sharon had been making cakes, only not in her own kitchen. Every time she thought that she might have begun to remember, another question popped into her head. It was so hard to try and piece things together. She knew it had been raining. *The worst storm ever, but what had that got to do with anything?* The effort involved in thinking was exhausting and soon Annie fell back into a deep sleep and there she re-discovered her friend.

Christine moved into the street when she was seven months' pregnant with Sharon. Her husband Peter was away somewhere fighting as a soldier in the war which had been raging for almost two years. So, they were born next door to each other, Annie the oldest by three days.

Mum said in those days before the National Health Service began you had to pay to see a doctor. There was a lady called Mrs Marriott who lived in the next street, who, for a small fee, would come and deliver your baby. Annie at seven years old thought that Mrs Marriott was a witch. She was always dressed in black and wore a strange looking hat with strings fastening under her chin. Christine agreed that she'd also been scared of Mrs Marriott but had been sent to fetch her when Mum went into labour and she was very kind. Christine had added "When you see her again you should say 'Hello' and then you'll see for yourselves what a lovely person she is." With that, Christine had dismissed us to play, adding that she didn't want to hear any more nonsense about witches.

Right from their first meeting, Mum had been friends with Christine, and their friendship lasted the rest of their lives and so, naturally, Annie and Sharon went everywhere together and some people even thought that they were sisters because they were always together.

Annie could only remember bits and bobs about the war, like always being told to eat everything from her plate as they didn't know where the next meal would be coming from. This was never a problem because they were always hungry and food shortages lasted for years after the war ended.

During the war, Grandma and Granddad had evacuees, two boys from London, as it was dangerous to live there with all the bombs being dropped. Sometimes Annie and Barbara would go to stay a few days. Unbeknown to them, this was because Mum was ill. Grandma used to make Desperate Dan's Cow Pie, named after the comic character. Grandma made the pie in a large vitreous enamel bowl with a thing in the middle, which looked like a duck's head, to let out the steam. The pastry crust was very thick. "To fill you lot up," Grandma used to say, adding sternly, "and if anybody finds any meat, I want to know about it." At the time the children didn't know there was actually no meat in it, just potatoes, onions and other vegetables from Granddad's garden. Still, they enjoyed every mouthful, and never left anything on their plates. Annie grinned at this thought, because there was not much on the plate in the first place.

The thought of food ushered Annie's mind to the end of the war when there was a big street party. All the children had been instructed to carry items to trestle tables, borrowed from the church hall, set out in a long line and covered with newspaper prettified with little pots of flowers and tiny Union Jack flags stuck into the tiny potatoes everyone called *pig taters*, as it was said that they were only fit for pigs to eat. The sun had been bright and hot in a cloudless sky. Very soon all the children were seated and being waited on by the women. Noticeably, there were hardly any men back from the fighting. Union Jack flags were everywhere and bunting flapped in the gentle breeze. Christine had made her special cakes using eggs which we brought back earlier from our Granddad's chickens. Then there was blancmange, deliciously pink, and Annie licked her lips at the thought of it.

After the food had been eaten and the tables cleared away, they had played games with all the grown-ups joining in. It was sad to see some of the women were crying for their husbands or sons.

Annie's Granddad made everyone laugh, blackening his face with soot and singing as he moved through the party, "Mama, I'd walk a million miles for one of your smiles." Everyone cheered and clapped. Perhaps he sang some more, but it was such a long time ago that Annie couldn't remember but they did stay up really late, until it was dark and everyone was singing Vera Lynn songs.

But what had these memories got to do with anything? Annie's thoughts turned to growing up.

Christine was lovely, always finding time for the children and a ready supply of cakes. She had light mousey brown hair that was always cropped short, making Annie believe, as a child, that it never grew. Her light brown eyes were always smiling and Annie loved to spend time at their house.

Sharon's Dad Peter was also great fun. He had a rounded belly which Christine said was cuddly. His greying hair had waves in it and he always had it cut short. He was clean-shaven and Sharon told Annie he was the most handsome Dad ever. He was always joking and making them laugh. He was good at card tricks but never revealed how any had worked and instigated water fights in his garden, which was nothing like Annie's with its neat flower beds and vegetable patches. No, Peter's idea of a garden was just grass, sprinkled with dandelions, much to the annoyance of Annie's Dad when the seeds blew over the fence. Peter had a job as a sales rep, working away from home for weeks at a time, so mowing the grass was left to Christine, and it was not a chore she wasted much energy on.

When Peter came home he always brought Sharon wonderful presents. For her eighth birthday, there was a huge dolls' house. At other times his gifts would be teddy bears, or jewellery, or miniature furniture for her dolls' house which she shared with Annie. Once Peter gave Annie a present which she treasured, a monkey on a ladder, and when you squeeze the bottom rungs together, it made the monkey do all kinds of acrobatic tricks. Sharon and Annie played with it for hours at a time. Peter also bought them a kaleidoscope, a tube containing pretty coloured tiny stones or glass which made the most wonderful patterns to view through a tiny hole, another toy to be treasured. Annie mused, *I wonder what became of them.*

Annie's favourite thing was to read her many books. Her older sister, Barbara, would read out loud to Mum when she was learning to read and Annie would sit with her and watch as her finger pointed to the words. Soon, Annie remembered all the words, and could read before she started school and one of her favourite trips was to the library where after Mum had chosen her books she would take them into the children's section to choose one each. Christine and Sharon came too, but Sharon was less keen on reading than drawing. She was good at painting too and her Mum framed some of her pictures and put them up on her bedroom wall.

Their lives were really happy as children. Even if their parents never had much money, they spent a lot of time on them. When they were skipping in the street, it would not be long before they had adults turning the rope or joining in their other games, a cricket match or a game of football. Of course, there were no parked cars preventing playing in the street.

Sharon and Annie started school together at five, and by then Barbara was allowed to take them for walks. They were sometimes allowed a few custard cream biscuits. Annie's mouth watered just at the thought of them and, in her sleep, she licked her lips. In the corner of a brown paper bag there might have been treasured cocoa and sugar to dip the biscuits into and, with this treat, they were in heaven.

Barbara took Sharon and Annie off across the fields and into the woods to pick wild flowers. The idea was to take them home as a present for their Mums, but after a while they tired of carrying them and put them by the wayside for collection on the way back, an intention seldom fulfilled.

They used to drink water from a spring flowing from a hole in the rock and then cascading down into a small stream, managing to get their clothes wet. They'd take off their shoes and socks to paddle and try to catch sticklebacks, scoop out frogspawn or pick up *water boatmen*, the beetles which used their legs like oars on a rowing boat.

Barbara made up stories like their Mum. The newts they found had been dropped to Earth from another planet and the lumps on their backs were where they had landed heavily. Annie liked newts, and never wanted to put them back in the water, but Barbara insisted that if they didn't, then they would die.

As they got older, they were allowed to wander on their own. Sometimes, there would be a gang of children down there, especially in the school holidays. One day, someone had tied a rope swing to a tree branch at the edge of a sheer drop. They only used it once. On their next visit it was gone, cut down, it was said because a girl had slipped and injured herself, flying scarily through the air.

For Annie childhood came back easily in her dreams...

They used to tie string around the top of empty jam jars as carrying handles and one day Sharon and Annie brought back jars of frog spawn and tipped them down a grate halfway down the wall of the big old house near the bottom of Annie's garden. They had long forgotten doing it when Mrs Warren began screaming in her cellar and brought everyone running. The girls peering down through the grill were spotted by the woman's husband. "I bet you two know something about this," he shouted, "just make your way round here and help me clear them up."

Mr Warren gave them buckets and made them spend an enjoyable hour chasing about after all the frogs.

Granddad came for tea and he chuckled and said he'd have loved to have seen Janet's face when she discovered the frogs. Annie's Dad told him not to encourage them. Annie asked how so many frogs came out and he said because the cellar was damp, the spawn turned into frogs and they were able to survive and multiply. Just like Janet and Joe, the appropriately named Warrens. Mum cuffed Granddad about the ear, "Stop winding her up," she chided. Annie loved her Granddad, who always made time for her and always found something to make her and Sharon laugh.

Annie smiled in her sleep.

4

Annie's friendship with Sharon became the stuff of her dreams.

After taking the eleven plus, they moved to senior school together and for the first time ever they saw a banana. They looked at it, wondering what to do with it. Their new teacher had managed to get one each for the whole of the class. What a treat! He said not to eat the yellow skin, just the white fruit inside, but they still spent ages looking at it, wondering what to do with it.

Sharon was always getting into trouble and dragging Annie in with her. They had not been at their new school many weeks when Sharon started falling out with everyone and on occasion even started to shout at Annie to get lost. Annie could not understand the change in her and complained to her Mum who sat her down and said to her as kindly as she could, "Peter has left Christine for another woman. I'm afraid Christine has gone to pieces over this too and has started drinking heavily. I'll do my level best to help her through this but Sharon's just lashing out at you because she's unhappy. You must both try your very best to support her until she can get back on track."

Annie nodded, not really knowing what she could do to help. Then when she thought things could not get any worse between them, Sharon began to mix with some of the rougher girls, completely ignoring her. They were always shouting and swearing and smoking. It was awful to watch what was happening to her friend. Sharon was getting into more and more trouble at school – if she actually went to school at all – and her horrible little gang were carrying out shoplifting sprees. They were stuffing booty into their socks, and then going to the cash desk to pay for one item so that the owner of the shop would not get suspicious.

On this one particular evening Annie decided to go and see Sharon at her house when she was on her own, away from the gang. Christine told her to go straight up as Sharon was in her bedroom. Sharon looked up from where she was lying on the bed reading a magazine and scowled, telling Annie to go. Annie told her that she had no intention of going and tried to convince her it was wrong to keep shoplifting because if she was caught she would now be old enough to go to prison.

"I don't care what happens to me," Sharon yelled. "Why don't you mind your own business, Miss Goody Two Shoes, and get out of my bedroom!"

Bolstered by what her Mum had said the other day Annie persevered, "Can you tell me what's happened to make you like this?"

"What do you care?" Sharon's voice was a little less loud than before.

"I care very much."

Without any warning Sharon began to cry. "It's all my fault," she blurted between sobs.

"What is?" Annie put her arm around her friend's shoulders.

"Dad's leaving."

"How can it be?" Annie asked.

"You don't want to know anyone as evil as me, so just go away," Sharon said angrily.

"I'm not going anywhere. You're my best friend whatever you've done, I'll still be your friend." Annie began to cry too.

When they were both much calmer, Annie tried again. "Tell me," she coaxed.

"I heard Mum on the phone to Dad. I could only hear what Mum was saying and she raised her voice, but she had no idea I was listening. She said, 'Are you saying that it's your little angel who's the cause of all this trouble? How dare you? You should be ashamed.'

"Then Dad said something and Mum said, 'In that case you'd better not show your face around here again. I'm not having you upsetting our Sharon with such a load of nonsense.' Then she slammed the phone down and went into the other room. She had no idea that I'd heard her say that it was all my fault. So, go away, I've split up my Mum and Dad, I'm so horrible." Then she cried again, taking in great gulps of air with her sobs.

Annie sat there holding her until an idea came to her. "Come on Sharon, my Mum will know what to do."

Sharon took a lot of coaxing, but eventually she told Annie's Mum everything, and Mum never said a word as she listened to Sharon tell her about the phone conversation she had overheard. Then Mum said, "Just give me a minute while I tell Jack where I'm going."

When she came back out she took Sharon with one hand and Annie with the other. "Come on," she ordered, "we're going to settle this once and for all." She led them back round to see Christine who was sitting in the lounge with a half empty bottle of wine.

The worst thing for Sharon had been that her Mum didn't seem to care what was happening. Christine had stopped cooking, cleaning her house, or doing any washing or ironing. Mum walked across the room and took the bottle away from Christine saying angrily, "Now listen to what this child has to say and don't interrupt until she's finished." She made Sharon repeat what she'd first told Annie and then herself.

Christine looked at her daughter through blurry eyes and then struggled to stand up and put her arms around her. Tears were running down her face as she kept saying sorry. Christine could hardly stand, having drunk so much, but she managed to say "I'm so sorry. I've been so wrapped up in my own misery that I never thought what it was doing to you. Your Dad had been seeing this other woman for years. That was why he spent so much time supposedly out on the road. When he didn't come home, he was with her."

Sharon interrupted, "But the phone call..."

"I'm coming to that," slurred Christine. "What you heard was his excuse for leaving us when he didn't want to. He said he couldn't be without his little angel. He has a two-year-old daughter; can you believe it? I need a drink."

Christine reached over for the bottle, but Mum spotted her move and took it away. "No, you don't. You need to put your Sharon straight first."

"Your Dad always called you his little princess, not his angel Sharon, so when you heard me telling him not to blame her, I meant his other daughter, not you my darling. You've done absolutely nothing wrong. Come here and give me a hug." Sharon ran to her Mum and they were both hugging each other when Mum nodded to Annie to leave them to it.

The next day Annie's Mum went to see Christine when the girls were at school. "Right. Get ready, we're going shopping."

"I can't," declared Christine. With great effort, she had been up since the crack of dawn. Washing was out on the line, and the house was spick and span again. Annie's Mum wouldn't take no for an answer and said she had got all day and would sit there until Christine agreed to come with her. Before too long Christine got washed and changed into something decent.

They did a little shopping, although Christine was short of money since Peter had gone. Then they went for a coffee in a small coffee shop they'd never frequented before. Mum went to the counter for the drinks and brought back a slice of cake each. Grudgingly, Christine began to sip her drink and Annie's Mum just kept smiling.

"What?" Christine demanded angrily. "There's nothing to smile for."

"Yes, there is. You have a beautiful daughter you adore. You have me as a friend, even if you have been ignoring me. So what if Peter has left you? It's his loss don't you think, not yours?"

Christine stirred her coffee before taking a bite of the cake. "Ugh! This is awful. What are you trying to do to me, Doreen? I thought that we were supposed to be best friends!"

Annie's Mum passed her a serviette to wipe her mouth. Then, smiling again, she said, "That's why I brought you here. They need someone to bake for them. Our Barbara went to school with Josie, the owner, and she asked me to bring you here because I told her you make 'exceedingly' good cakes."

Christine reached over the table to squeeze Annie's Mum's hand. "Thank you," she mouthed, afraid to speak out loud in case she burst into tears.

Josie came over to their table to join them then. "Doreen has told me great things about you Christine, so don't let her down. Can you start tomorrow at seven? We can talk about your hours and your pay then, unless you'd rather we do it now?"

Hardly able to speak, Christine nodded to Josie, mumbling, "Tomorrow."

As they left the tea shop, Christine kept saying "Thank you, thank you. I'm so sorry, I'm sorry," over and over again.

Annie's Mum said there was no need to say that and they linked arms to walk to the bus stop.

This was the turning point. Christine had a job doing what she loved and she soon put Sharon back on the straight and narrow so she never had anything more to do with the gang.

It wasn't that Sharon never got into trouble again, but it wasn't the same.

When it was their third year Staff versus School football match, since neither of them liked football, Sharon suggested that they go into a classroom to do their homework in advance. Then they could go out that night. The connecting classrooms had been army billets during the war with a door at each end so that you could walk along through at least five rooms. Sharon was first to hear approaching footsteps and grabbed her things and hid in a cupboard. Annie was left crouching down in a corner behind a pile of chairs. Fortunately, it was two prefects who had been dating, and only had eyes for each other, so Annie wasn't spotted.

The next interruption though was a teacher, Mr Hayward. The girls ran for the opposite door, but someone else's footsteps were coming from that direction too. Annie bunked Sharon up, so she could climb through an open window but she had no chance of getting out herself.

Mr Hayward rushed to the window but didn't see anyone else. He gave Annie a detention which meant staying after school the next night. However, this was Annie's third detention that term so she knew she'd also have to see the Head Master. Later Mr Hayward came to give her one more chance to tell him who had been in the classroom with her but Annie continued to maintain she was alone.

Then the teacher surprised her completely by letting her off the detention for being so loyal to her friend. He said that Sharon had been to him and confessed that it was all her fault, as the one who'd persuaded Annie to go into the classroom.

Annie knew she was lucky to have such a friend and they remained friends for the rest of their lives.

5

In a flash, childhood had gone and Annie was walking with two friends in hot summer sunshine, which never seemed to fade. She was older, probably about eighteen. Sharon was laughing with the other girl, Angela, who worked with Annie. Angela was so easy to get on with. Annie's Dad always said that you go to work to earn money, and if you enjoyed it, so much the better. They were enjoying it too.

Sharon worked in an office down the road so they were able to travel to and from work together. Becoming firm friends, they also socialised going to lots of different places together. They tried to ice-skate at the city rink without much success and found it rather too expensive, especially adding in the bus fare both ways.

On a particular day, they were outside a local Coffee Bar trying to decide whether to go in or not, when three handsome young men passed them heading inside. They looked at each other, and as was the way with young girls, giggled to each other and turned to follow them in.

Annie suddenly stopped dead in her tracks. "I'm not allowed in here. My Dad heard about some youths fighting outside last week, and the police being called to break it up."

"That's it then," declared Sharon. "We'll just have to watch as someone else gets one of those hunks." She was the flirt amongst them, flashing her amazing hazel eyes with the black rings defining them. It was always the first thing people noticed about her but she had other advantages. She had natural blonde hair, which she wore long. She would shake her head to make it billow around her face and her trim figure always turned heads even if she pretended not to notice.

Annie said, "You two go ahead and I'll catch up with you later."

"No way," said Angela. "We'll all keep together. What's that saying, all for one and one for all, remember, the three musketeers."

The others thought that Angela was sharp with all her sayings. She had been brought up by her Grandma and had inherited some funny little ways, but she had a heart of gold. Her auburn hair was naturally curly and she had a job ever getting it untangled. She had brown eyes and a face covered in freckles. Angela was also taller than the others. She used to say she got that from her father, but Annie and Sharon knew that she had never met him. She didn't even have photographs of her parents. Apparently, her Mum had left Angela with her Grandma for a few days when she was a baby, so that she and her current boyfriend, Angela's father, could go away for a short holiday. They never came back for her and when her Grandma checked, she found her daughter had taken all her belongings with her. She obviously had had no intention of returning for her baby. Angela's Grandma said she was better off without her Mum and that was that. Angela was a very happy girl and her Grandma adored her. Perhaps unsurprisingly, Angela never formed any notion of finding out what had happened to her natural parents.

Annie was a contrast to both the others with short mousey brown hair, which had been styled in the same way forever, and a more rounded figure; not fat exactly but certainly not skinny. Her eyes were mostly green but with a strong hint of grey. Her Mum used to say that she could tell what the weather was going to be like by the colour of Annie's eyes, green for a sunny day and grey for a dull one. She was also on occasion easily led and now feeling a killjoy she relented. "You have to back me up if Dad finds out."

Sharon said "I'll say it was my fault because I felt faint and we only went in to get a drink of water." By way of emphasis, she raised the back of her hand dramatically to her forehead. They all laughed and sauntered into the Coffee Bar as if they owned the place.

It was quite dark inside and it took a while to get used to the dimmed lighting. Loud music was playing from a Juke Box in the corner. There were little lights glittering from what looked like a giant fishing net fastened onto the wall and covered with sea shells. Huge, pretend spiders hung from the ceiling on rope webs. Annie shuddered; even fake spiders gave her the shivers. When their eyes got used to the dimness, they became aware that skeletons were standing in every nook and cranny.

The boys were nowhere to be seen. They ordered soft drinks and slid onto bench seats at an empty table. They were looking around, nudging each other and giggling, when one of the lads appeared. He came straight over and asked if they'd been in before, as he hadn't seen them. They shyly told him that this was their first time.

Annie was absorbed in the surroundings when she was brought back sharply. "Budge up," the boy said to Sharon. "Make room for a little 'un."

Sharon obediently slid along the seat, and Patrick, as he introduced himself, sat down beside her. He said that they could call him Paddy as his friends did and a few minutes later those friends came to join them.

Eric was at least six feet tall, with the most piercing blue eyes and an attractive smile showing a set of pearly white teeth. His dark brown hair was brushed back, as was the fashion, into what was known as *a DA*. He squeezed into the bench seat next to Annie.

This left Angela with Tom. He was quite a joker, and soon had them in stitches about some of their exploits. He told them about a trip on the Norfolk Broads on a boat. They had tied up for the night and gone off to the nearest pub for a pint. The way he said it was *a pint or six*. Anyway, they found their befuddled way back to the boat and all sparked out. They didn't wake up even though things were falling from the shelves. When they finally did, they thought that they'd been burgled and that they must still be drunk, as none of them could stand up. Tom said he got to the door first and started laughing and laughing. "Well," he said, "we tied up the boat too tight and the tide had gone out so we're left hanging there with most of the boat out of the water. So, we all scrambled up the bank and stood there wondering what to do."

"I suggested cutting the ropes," said Paddy.

"Then there was this runner going by. He told us to sit tight because the tide was already coming back in."

There were other stories. Lots of them and all hilarious. They left the Coffee Bar to walk home by the side of the river. It had been a wonderful afternoon running into the early evening but it was to be only the first of Annie's meetings with Eric. He took her home that first evening, after being warned not to mention where they'd met to Annie's Dad.

They spent lots of time together over the next two years even though at first, neither of Annie's parents had been too keen on him. He was clever with his hands and worked in a garage and often called for her still wearing his boiler suit having come straight from work. Annie's parents thought she should be looking for someone with good prospects and her elder sister, Barbara, told her it had been the same for her; nobody was good enough for their daughters. Mum and Dad had eventually come around and a wedding was being planned for the next time Simon got army leave but he never did come home from the Korean War, and she hadn't found anyone to come close to how she had felt about him. This was the first time her big sister had confided in Annie who felt enormously privileged. Barbara said not to worry about Mum and Dad's views.

Annie wasn't worried. It was unimportant to her what they thought, because she and Eric were in love and no one was going to split them up. *That was youth for you.*

They walked everywhere in those days because neither of them had much money to spend on going out. Occasionally, they went for motorbike rides, sometimes joined by the rest of the gang.

Angela didn't date Tom for long and he went into the army after they split up. She had another boyfriend soon afterwards called Ralph. He was better suited to Angela, his more serious nature complementing her happy go lucky streak. It turned out that Ralph had been a friend of Eric's for years and sometimes they all went to the cinema, and now and again to a local dance together.

6

For a dreaming Annie, those times and the life-long friendships they had forged were very real and then she remembered the day when Eric proposed after they'd been seeing each other for over two years. On this particular day they had gone out for a ride on his motorbike and had stopped to admire the beauty of the view with the overnight frost still keeping the grass white. He suddenly turned to her and said, "Would you like to marry me?"

For Annie looking up into his piercing blue eyes was the clincher. "Of course, I would."

Eric said, "I'm glad you said yes. I don't think I'd be able to get a refund on this." From his pocket, he pulled a blue box and inside was an engagement ring. "I've been saving up," he said. "That's one of the reasons we've been doing a lot of walking lately." He slipped the ring onto her finger, and it fitted perfectly. He said, "I cheated a bit. I borrowed your cameo ring and took it to the shop with me."

"Very clever," Annie teased and kissed him.

Eric said, "I've got the opportunity to buy my own garage and a house comes with it. It'll need modernising but we can do that gradually."

Just talking about it made it seem almost a reality, and after a while, they realised the sun was setting over the beautiful view that from now on would always be their place. Annie shivered. It was getting cold. "Can you do something for me, Eric?"

"Anything for you, my sweet," he said.

"You haven't heard what it is yet."

"Spit it out then."

"Well, you know how old fashioned my Dad is."

"Yerrs," drawled Eric.

"Well, would you ask his permission before we tell anyone?"

"For you darling I will. Although your Dad frightens the life out of me."

Eric spoke to Annie's Dad the next day, and the funny thing was that once he was going to be his son-in-law they became great friends.

By the time of their rather quiet wedding in early May, they had saved the deposit for the garage and both sets of Mums and Dads gave them cheques for wedding presents which would further reduce what they'd need to borrow from the bank.

The weather was glorious. Annie's dress came with a long train. It was *old and borrowed*, as was the tradition, from her sister, who insisted she have it, reminding her, with a tearful smile, that it had never been used, so could also be said to be *something new*. She was much thinner than Annie so they let it out and Mum sewed hundreds of sequins onto the train to sparkle when she moved.

Sharon and Angela, who were the bridesmaids, laughingly presented Annie with a *blue* garter to complete the required traditional set. Eric wore his best suit having taken it to be dry-cleaned. "It would be a waste of money to buy a new one as I hardly ever wear one anyway." He could have come in his boiler suit as far as Annie was concerned, just so long as he didn't leave her standing alone at the altar. "That was never going to happen," he told her afterwards.

They were married on the Saturday, moved straight into their new house and were both at work on the Monday. There was no honeymoon, only the shared promise of a holiday together later when they could afford it.

The house was definitely in need of some modernisation, but as money was tight, they scrubbed and cleaned what they could and made do. It surprised them how generous their friends and neighbours could be and they soon made the place inhabitable.

They dipped into their savings to buy a bed and basic furniture. The huge kitchen had a big fireplace with a boiler on one side, which heated the water, and the oven on the other side. There was a large front entrance hall with doors leading off into two other good-sized rooms. They also had gas lighting which seemed very romantic at first, but they soon found out how difficult it was to buy gas mantles and it took the romance out of it when you had to use a candle or walk around in the dark. Eric had a friend who, for a sensible price, wired up the house for electricity once they'd saved up enough to pay him. In the winter, for many years before the days of central heating, they got used to having ice on the inside of the windows of the bedrooms which made pretty patterns like exotic trees. They used to say that Jack Frost had been up in the night to draw them.

Annie's Grandma gave them a washing machine. It was an old one, but it was much better than washing by hand or carting things to the launderette. Then they had the fireplace taken out as there was no way to produce a decent meal using the old oven. They bought an Aga cooker, which also gave them hot water and it was Annie's pride and joy. She found she loved to cook and became quite proficient over the years if never quite as good with cakes as Sharon's Mum.

The house had a small laundry room but more importantly an inside toilet which so excited Annie for whom taking that long walk out of the back door had been a nightmare in the winter. There were also three large bedrooms and an upstairs bathroom. When Eric dramatically whipped open the door to show Annie, she was ecstatic with the luxury of it all and rewarded Eric with a big hug.

The front step had been carefully scrubbed, probably for decades, and then finished off with Cardinal Red, a kind of polish. Early on a passing neighbour commented to Annie that you could tell a lot about a person when you saw how clean their step was. She shrugged not then understanding how snobbish some people could be.

Eric loved his garage, working very long hours, and sometimes returning only after Annie was asleep. He was always hungry and somehow expected her to keep his food warm for hours. She had only just learnt to cook dinners properly to get everything ready at the same time, so he had no chance of her keeping it both hot and fresh. Pragmatically they settled on a routine by which he would leave what he was doing at around six o'clock, eat his dinner and then go back if he needed to. This worked better in those long-ago days pre-microwave ovens.

It wasn't long before Annie was pregnant.

The thought of her pregnancy made Annie wake up. She somehow knew that she had remembered something very important from the past. With a struggle, she sat up. She suddenly knew that the women were pregnant and that her sister Barbara was in charge of delivering their babies. *How could this be so? Surely the women would have had a young midwife, not an old woman. Why weren't they in the hospital to have their babies?* Everything was so difficult to comprehend. Every idea threw up another question. *Who were these mothers? How did they fit into the reason why her memory had gone? Why did Eric come into everything and why isn't he here to help me sort things out?* Annie put her head in her hands as she tried to unravel her thoughts, but the effort proved too much, and again she swayed about and slumped heavily back on the sheepskin bed.

Sleep reclaimed her and Annie's thoughts jumped back to her first pregnancy.

Money was tight, normal enough for a new business. It would take time to get established with regular customers, Eric always said.

Annie's Dad bought the pram for his first grandchild. They ended up having four children in quick succession, and the same pram lasted them all. Joanne was born first. She had a peaches and cream complexion and piercing blue eyes, like her Dad's, encased in the longest dark eyelashes. Annie used to say to herself that she'll never need mascara. She was a good baby and Annie couldn't understand other women at the clinic where their babies were checked and weighed, complaining so much about their offspring.

A year later, Thomas was born. *What a difference!* He cried for no apparent reason and he kept them awake night after night. Eric maintained that he had to go to work the next day whereas Annie could catch up on her sleep during the day and so he stayed in bed leaving Annie to leap out when Thomas cried. It was years later when Annie was ill for about a week, and he had to look after the children, that he saw just how daft his views had been.

Annie tried every recommendation her mother and friends could suggest, but still Thomas wailed. When Thomas was eighteen months old and Annie was pregnant with John she was beside herself with weariness and despair. *If she had another baby who cried as much as Thomas, then how could she cope?*

When the new baby arrived and John was introduced to Joanne and Thomas, Annie was in dread as to how Thomas would take this intrusive newcomer. After all he had demanded and received Annie's undivided attention from the day he was born. She was in for a very pleasant surprise. Thomas poked the baby with a fat wet finger he had just taken from his mouth.

"Baby," he said as he poked John gently. "My baby." From that day on, they were inseparable and Thomas stopped crying. "Only babies cry."

By the time that their youngest daughter Jane was born, the others were at school, so it was just like having an only child until the others came bounding home to complete their happy family.

They bought a caravan and had lots of short breaks, not going far, but always enjoying ourselves. The only frustration was getting the van packed up ready for a weekend away only to find that a customer's car was short of a spare part which would not be available until Saturday morning, or some other problem job materialised so they had to postpone their trip. Eric never could understand why this could possibly annoy Annie so much. "Don't be cross," he would say, "I have to earn a living."

After a while, Annie got the hang of not mentioning to the children that they were possibly going so as not to disappoint them and then stocking up the freezer with baking so that it was just a five-minute job to transfer the food into the fridge in the caravan, once Eric gave her the definite go! They had some great times. One favourite spot was by the river, on a small campsite where the owner always found space for them no matter how full it seemed to be. The children could paddle in the river's shallows. There was a huge stone in the middle and as they got braver, sometimes with their Dad holding their hand, the children would stand triumphantly on it as if they had just climbed Mount Everest.

They bought a blow-up dinghy and Eric took each of them in turn for a trip down the river. It was not very deep but they fished for trout and occasionally caught one big enough to eat and laughter abounded.

The children grew up without much difficulty, getting on remarkably well with each other. Of course, there were squabbles but they never lasted long. They had spats with their friends at school sometimes, but, before things required sorting out with the parents, the children had usually made it up and were again best friends. Kids have a way of sorting out most of their childhood difficulties, without the help of adults. Annie and Eric always told them there was nothing that their Mum or Dad couldn't sort out and the children seemed to rub along nicely enough.

The only dark time was when Annie was about thirty years old and a terrible motorway accident claimed the lives of Eric's Mum and Dad. He was devastated and fell into an overwhelming depression which lasted until one day the children came bounding in from school and playfully leapt on their Dad. He was so angry and the children were confused and hurt. Later that same day, Eric apologised for how he had been behaving and said he felt bad about taking it out on the children. The loss of their grandparents was hardly their fault after all. From then on Eric was back to his old self. Just occasionally, Annie would catch him staring into space with a sad look on his face, but with determination, he did overcome his grief. As they say, time is a great healer. The children were more and more the focus of his and their lives and, in short, they were a very close-knit family.

One afternoon Eric came home from work early. He had a problem with one of the vehicles and thought he'd think about the problem overnight instead of getting wound up about it. On the radio a new tune was playing. *"These boots are made for walking."* Eric was usually a very serious sort of person, but he started to dance around the garden pulling such peculiar faces as he danced around that tears of laughter ran down Annie's face and all the children got up and joined in. When the music stopped, they all fell in a convulsing heap. The moment passed and Eric said "What's for tea?"

This, for some reason, set Annie off again into peals of laughter.

The children worked hard at their schoolwork and all of them did well. Maybe if they had had the sort of parents who really pushed them, they'd have received higher grades, but they belonged to a family in which happiness trumped achievement. They were well disciplined though as Eric wouldn't stand for any nonsense. Annie's input was mainly to teach them to be well mannered, how to read, and personal hygiene. "Courtesy costs nothing," she would say.

When John was about eleven years old, he came running in from school quite out of breath. "Hello Mum," he said. "Now we'll be dead."

"What on Earth are you going on about?" Annie asked him.

He explained they had been discussing the four-minute warning we would receive if Nuclear Rockets had been fired at our country. "I would only just be able to get home if running as fast as I can," he said. Since he'd had to cross a busy main road to get home, Annie was very worried that he should even be thinking this way and assured him this kind of thing wouldn't happen as the Government had everything under control

John was unconvinced. "What about the flu epidemic at the end of the First World War? The Government of the day said that it wouldn't reach us, but it did and it killed hundreds of people."

Annie had no answer to this and told him to wash his hands ready for tea but later that evening, John resurrected the subject.

Eric said, "This is a way the Government has of keeping the public on edge. We're like pawns in a game of chess; dispensable. We've had the scare about Communists and that didn't develop into anything, so why should we be worried about rockets? We've been told that there would be a pandemic with just about every type of flu and nothing's happened." Eric was just getting started. "Yes, some of them may have reached epidemic proportions in some parts of the world, before fizzling out, but I think the scare stories were just a way of keeping us under threat and in our place all the time."

John was about to interrupt but his Dad continued. "We can't do anything about the rockets anyway, because if they come, then they come, but you can do something about getting your homework done, so off you go." John groaned but knew that as far as his Dad was concerned that was the end of the conversation.

It didn't take long anyway before John stopped worrying about rockets and for something new to catch his imagination because Eric came in from work, and as he was changing out of his wet boiler suit; it was soaking because it had been non-stop rain all day; he grinned and asked if they'd like a holiday in Spain.

"Well," Annie said prodding the boiler suit into the washing machine, "...the weather has got to better than it is here."

"That's settled then," Eric said, and after putting on a fresh boiler suit, went back to work leaving Annie and the children bewildered.

That night after the children were tucked up in bed, Eric told Annie that as the school holidays were starting next week, he had asked Peter to look after things while they went away for a fortnight. "Peter's been working for me long enough now and he's quite capable of running the place for a couple of weeks. So, lass, all you have to do is pack and we'll be off."

"Where are we going to stay?" Annie asked tentatively.

"In a tent," said Eric. "I bought one last week. Didn't I tell you?"

Annie was stunned. Never in her wildest dreams had she suspected Eric of possessing such a wild sense of adventure.

As it turned out it was the beginning of a new era in their lives. They all returned from Spain exhilarated. It had proved such a success that they were already talking about where to head off to the next year. After that they headed for the sun every year until the children were ready to leave home.

7

Again, Annie stirred in her sleep, recollecting the happy times they had had in Spain, but she was too exhausted to wake up.

She smiled to herself, as something else came to her mind, the time when Joanne, her oldest daughter, had gained a little weight. Annie remembered telling her it was only *puppy fat* and it would go when she was older. One evening Joanne came home from school having been on the receiving end of three boys making nasty remarks about her being fat. She had been losing the battle of words and was close to tears when out of nowhere her little brother, John, arrived. Physically he was no match for the older boys but gave them such a mouthful that it sent them reeling. John's explanation was that it was alright for anyone in the family to call Joanne fat if they wanted to, but he wasn't going to stand by and let anyone else say it.

"If that's what you think, then I'm watching what I eat from now on," yelled Joanne. She was really upset.

"Perhaps it'd be a good idea if you also took up a sport," said Tom.

"That will do boys," Annie said.

Both brothers grabbed hold of her and playfully tipped and tapped, joyfully pulling and pushing their sister around and cackling all the time until eventually Joanne had to laugh too.

"Take no notice," said Tom, when they eventually stopped tormenting her. "We're only messing. You look fine to me."

But, Joanne did take notice. She ate less stuff like crisps and joined the school tennis team. Within a short time, she shed a few pounds and one of the boys who had been having a go at her asked her out on a date to the pictures. He told her he was sorry but had only been trying to get her attention because she never gave him a second glance.

This was the start of something new in their lives. There were now always lots of friends of both sexes at their house. All their children seemed popular although John said the reason was "Because you make lovely cakes Mum."

In Annie's sleep it seemed no time at all before John met and married a sweet young woman called Amanda. Annie remembered thinking Amanda didn't look old enough to be getting married with her long corn coloured hair plaited or bound with pretty ribbons. There was not a blemish on her beautiful face and her unusual green eyes and slight lashes and eyebrows gave her the look of a child rather than of a young woman but then Amanda confided to Annie that this was going to be the first time in her life that she would be choosing to take a new surname; her Mum had married three times and Amanda had had to take on the surname of the new step-father each time. Now, she had no one, her Mum having died of a heart attack, "Not surprisingly given the amount of drugs she and *him* was always taking." Anyway, her last stepdad, *who incidentally was a waste of space, and never actually married my Mum*, had taken up with a woman who already had three children. He'd moved them into the house she had shared with her Mum before he came onto the scene and told Amanda to get lost. She ran straight into the protective arms of their John and she told Annie that she was the luckiest person alive to be marrying John, which brought more than a tear of sympathy to Annie's eyes.

Their wedding was a lovely affair. Annie did all the catering including making a three-tier cake. John wanted the reception at home and didn't go with the trend of hiring a disco. They invited all the family and the neighbours but everyone managed to find a seat in the house or out in the garden. John's best friend, Jed, read out the telegrams and made a short speech. He was very nervous but said that it was easier in familiar surroundings than it would have been in a strange place.

Of course, Annie and Eric's best friends, Paddy and Sharon, came with their son Patrick, who was the image of his Dad, and his girlfriend, a pretty young lady who was rather shy and held onto Patrick the whole time. Angela and Ralph had brought their only child, Linda. She didn't resemble either of her parents. She was very small compared to her Mum and hadn't a trace of auburn hair or curls. Angela said she had no idea who Linda took after since she had never known her parents.

Ralph joked, "I don't know where she came from; my parents are very tall with jet-black hair like me." Angela pushed him to admit the truth. "Okay, my Grandmother on my Dad's side was very tiny."

Linda also brought her fiancé. He was tall and smart and full of fun. A perfect match everyone told them.

Eric had put banners up in the garden and fixed wires outside so they could broadcast some music. Everyone had a brilliant time, although tinged with the little sadness of knowing that the bride and groom would soon be off to the other side of the world.

Annie woke again and looked around her. Tears were running down her face as she tried desperately to remember why John and Amanda migrating to Australia carried such dreadful foreboding for her. *What could possibly have happened to cause this dread?* They had been such a happy couple setting off to start a new life. She pulled herself up into a sitting position again. The name Dillon came into her mind. *Was that her daughter Joanne's husband? No, his name was Budd.* She shook her head, chastising herself for not remembering the name of her own son-in-law. *Who was Dillon then?* She racked her brain in frustration, flopping back down onto the sheepskin bed. No matter how hard she tried, she couldn't comprehend what could have caused her such grief.

Budd? Joanne married a Canadian Airman called Budd when he was serving at a nearby Airforce Base. He only managed two days' leave, so they got married in a Register Office and spent their honeymoon in married quarters on the Base. Joanne stayed in England for the three years of his contract during which time they had two children.

Thinking of them, Annie was both happy and perplexed, knowing that she would never see them again: her gorgeous grandchildren; Madison the youngest and cutest child imaginable with her light blonde hair and brilliant blue eyes and Bartram, named after his American Grandfather, the complete opposite – dark brown hair and thick-rimmed glasses disguising dark brown eyes, and so thin, which was surprising given the amount of junk food he always seemed to consume. He was always reading a book or using a games console and it was difficult to get him into a conversation but his school grades were always excellent and he was expected to achieve in whatever he chose to do.

Budd and Joanne had believed they would all get a better life in Canada so, soon after John emigrated, so did Joanne, leaving Annie and Eric to make the difficult adjustment of losing two of their children almost simultaneously. Of course, they had travelled to visit them both on several occasions, the last time being to celebrate Eric's retirement, and were planning well ahead to go to Australia for Christmas in a few years' time to celebrate their Golden Wedding Anniversary and to Canada the following summer.

Thomas, Annie and Eric's second-born, worked in a laboratory at the university and lived about ten miles away. Exceptionally clever, Thomas seemed to soak up information all through school and was a star pupil in science, winning an award for physics when he was in the third year for some kind of discovery he had made when doing experiments in the school lab. The science teacher used to stay after school to help him because he was so keen. He stayed on two extra years in higher education to get his master's degree and neither of his parents could even pretend to understand what he did for a living.

Sadly, Thomas lost his first wife Annette to cancer, when she was only twenty-three years old. She struggled so hard with it, but after six months in remission it came back more aggressively and there was nothing to be done. Thomas threw himself into work, spending long hours trying to create a breakthrough for bowel cancer, the disease which took away his wife. He worked so hard, and such long hours, that Annie feared for his own health. Then a new junior technician was taken on to work in his lab. She was bright and funny, and she gradually became the soul-mate their Thomas needed. They courted for a year and he asked her to marry him. Jenny said yes straight away. The age gap, eight years, didn't make any difference to her. They had a beautiful wedding and she looked a picture in the lovely dress which Jane made for her. It was a traditional, almost old-fashioned design, with a high neck. Sewn into the dress were artificial dropped pearls, so perfect they looked real. Jenny was overwhelmed when she first tried the dress on and was afraid to ask how much it had cost to make. Jane waved her fears aside and pointed out that designing was what she did for a living and since her company was branching out into wedding dresses, the chance to experiment was beneficial all round. The wedding was a quiet affair. Jenny's Mum organised everything and since neither family was very large they were all able to chat with each other instead of separating into a bride's side and a groom's clique.

Thomas and Jenny came to see Annie and Eric as often as they could and rang every week but there didn't seem to be enough hours in the day to achieve all Thomas wanted and having children wasn't a priority for them. Jenny said there was plenty of time and anyway she loved working with Thomas in the laboratory.

If they didn't see enough of Thomas, the same couldn't be said of Annie and Eric's youngest daughter. Jane and her husband Nigel lived only a half hour's drive away but they married so young that for two years they were grateful to take up Eric's suggestion of staying with them to save enough money to get onto the property ladder. Their daughter Rebecca was born in that time and in order for Jane to continue working, Annie agreed to look after the baby for three days a week while Nigel's Mum had her for the other two days. Fortunately, Rebecca was a good baby and always seemed to be smiling. She had the same dark eyes as her mother and long eyelashes which were always the first thing everyone seemed to comment on. The pleasure Annie took in seeing the baby grow in her charge made it a huge wrench when they finally left to move into their own house. That was a little bit too far away for Rebecca to stay with her Grandma while Jane was at work and she went to a nursery, where she had a terrific time interacting with all the other children. Jane loved her job and she was good at both the design and business sides and the company was soon selling clothes all over the world, many of them Jane's own designs.

Jane's husband Nigel was ideal in the roles of both father and husband. He was tall and had his head shaved, not just to be fashionable but because he was losing his hair anyway. It was obvious from the start of his relationship with Jane that he would love and protect her for the rest of his life. They would have liked more children, but it never happened. Nigel worked in the Council's finance department, wearing a smart suit and shirt and tie every day, and he too seemed satisfied with the challenges his work gave him.

Rebecca grew up into a wonderful young woman and after university where she met her future husband, Simon, they both worked in advertising, living in London. They were very busy people and couldn't come north to visit very often but now it seemed they were planning to apply for jobs in the Midlands and to buy a house nearer their Mum and Dad, meaning Annie and Eric would see much more of their granddaughter.

8

Annie was sleeping most of the time and her mind was flicking between the phases of her long life, pulling open the memories of each element in turn and now her thoughts touched on the years of their retirement.

The Langfords, Annie and Eric, were a long time married. They knew each other so well and cross words between them were a rarity even if occasional exasperation was not but somehow Eric always managed to wheedle his way around Annie. To celebrate Eric's retirement at sixty-five they had planned a trip to Australia to visit John and his wife Amanda, and their grandchildren Melanie and Stuart. Amanda had blossomed as a wife and mother and she always said that having her own identity was the best thing which could ever have happened to her. Now she was older with a few grey hairs showing but her face was still as beautiful and young-looking as ever.

Annie and Eric had a month in the Antipodes, three weeks of which were in Adelaide with John, Amanda and Melanie. Among other trips, they were taken to a zoo so massive they needed to be driven around it in a bus. There they saw endangered species, mostly from Africa. Annie had never realised that Giraffes were so big. There were Bison, the animals known as Buffalos slaughtered in their millions in the American Wild West and now a protected species in danger of extinction.

Melanie took Annie to the Art Gallery to spend hours looking at Aboriginal dot paintings among other things while Eric and John went to a site where they could look for opals although neither found any. Melanie and Annie got on well and seemed to understand each other without having to always put it into words. They hadn't seen much of their granddaughter over the years growing up, but to Annie it seemed as though they had only seen each other the day before.

Stuart, seven years older than his sister, lived on a Sheep Station in the middle of nowhere. Annie and Eric found to their surprise that there was little sign of any other people living in the vicinity and saw that the red, sandy panoramic view from the house contained precious little vegetation. Without warning them, though, Stuart had invited all his neighbours to a huge party to celebrate his grandparents' visit. People travelled miles to get there. Boards were laid down as a dance floor and out came the fiddles and soon everyone found themselves clapping their hands and stamping their feet as the caller shouted out instructions for one square dance after another. There was a massive barbeque with every type of food imaginable and Stuart introduced us to his latest girlfriend. She was very sweet and also a very small woman, but Stuart said not to let that deceive them because Chloe could keep up with any man when it came to shearing time. Chloe had very short cropped hair which gave her a boyish look, and twinkling eyes, especially when Stuart came near. Her accent caused some difficulty to the visitors as she had a broad Australian drawl.

At the end everyone came to say their individual goodbyes to Annie and Eric but the astonishing thing was that next morning when they came down to breakfast, there was no residual evidence that the party had even happened. Stuart told them clearing up was painstakingly undertaken to avoid encouraging dingoes or snakes to come in close to the house in search of food.

Later that year, Annie and Eric made the Canadian trip they'd planned, visiting The Great Lakes with Joanne and Budd, where Eric found a new talent for fly fishing, with the help of his son-in-law and grandson. There were more barbeques attended by friends who were fascinated by their English accents. There was sightseeing and because it was the school holidays, camping in Yellowstone Park where, at a safe distance, through binoculars, they watched Brown Bears catching fish in a river. Budd hired a dhingy so they could go out to one of the small islands where wildlife abounded and there were hides for bird watching.

Annie, deep into her memories of this wonderful time in Canada, turned over on her sheepskin bed and without warning her perspective shifted and she was back at home sitting in her favourite armchair. Eric was there too nodding contentedly in his chair and they were mulling over their trips abroad and reflecting on how lucky they were to have such a wonderful family.

Annie looked across at Eric. He seemed to have shrunk a little as he grew older, but still had all his hair although it was now grey instead of dark brown. His eyes had lost none of the sparkle which had attracted her all those years ago. He had kept himself fit with plenty of exercise, at work and latterly in their large garden. Eric glanced up and caught Annie scrutinising him. "What are you thinking?"

"Nothing much." Annie smiled.

At that moment Mary woke Annie up to give her a hot drink. She helped the old lady into a sitting position and held the mug out for her to sip. Annie asked if she had been asleep long. The sun was still bright and low in the sky making her think that it might be the next day. Mary drew a clock face on the ground and marked off one hour. Annie shrugged her shoulders as she thought of all the things which had passed through her mind in such a short space of dreaming. After sipping a little of the hot liquid, Annie indicated that she had needed to lie down again. Carefully, Mary helped her and moments later Annie was deeply asleep once more.

9

This time Annie's focus rested on her friends, Sharon and Angela, Paddy and Ralph. They had all been keen golfers in their younger days. Eric was always off for a game at every opportunity with his oldest friends, Paddy and Ralph, whereas Sharon and Annie only managed to play occasionally, when they could get someone to sit with the children. A couple called Jean and Les who lived lower down their street sometimes obliged. They didn't have children of their own and seemed happy to look after theirs. As it took such a long time to play a full round, the women mostly played in the summer evenings when the nights were lighter for longer and then they usually limited themselves to eight or ten holes. Their level of skill was not good by any stretch of the imagination and they joked that they got better value for money than the men because they ended up playing many more shots. Eventually things must have fallen into place because fourteen shots per hole became a reasonable six or seven.

Ralph and Angela lived nearby but Angela didn't play golf; she couldn't get the hang of it and always said that she didn't want to ruin a good walk. She was usually on hand when Sharon needed to leave their son with her so she could play golf. Years later Ralph had a heart attack and was advised to avoid stress and to give up golf for the time being. Their only grandchild, a boy, Philip, had spent much of his young life with them because his Mum and Dad had gone to work in Singapore and wanted him educated in England. He made his grandparents very proud when he graduated and went on to get a job with an eminent scientist in London.

Paddy and Sharon also lived a short walk away from us, and Paddy commuted to his job in the city. Their son had gone to live in Ireland, and their only granddaughter Siobhan spent most school holidays with her grandparents. Now she travelled the world for an English company and the last they heard was that she was in Mexico.

The six friends met up as often as possible and often spent weekends together, with or without grandchildren as an excuse for trips to the seaside, a theme park, or the zoo.

Eric and his keenness for his garden made the sleeping Annie smile. Since retirement, gardening was his main hobby. He had a greenhouse where he grew tomatoes, grapes, courgettes and cucumbers. Outside, he had a fruit cage full of every kind of fruit: gooseberries, blackcurrants, redcurrants, and raspberries just to name but a few. The rest of his garden was full of vegetables which kept them and even friends and neighbours supplied all year.

As Annie's thoughts unravelled, she recalled one exceptionally cold winter. "So much for Global Warming," Eric had grumbled. There had also been a lot of rain, forcing them to spend more time indoors. The strange weather was becoming even more a topic of conversation than usual. Over the last few years, there had been droughts and water had to be transported between areas while other places were inundated with water; flooding becoming a regular occurrence. One of the cheapest options for transporting water to the drought areas would be to open up the old canals but it would still cost millions to pay for the project. There are records of Irish Navvies digging the original canals by hand and some bright spark in Government suggested it would be a useful occupation for prisoners to be doing, instead of sitting in their cells, contributing nothing to the economy. Before long, the idea took shape and although unpopular with some, it was the start of something different. It probably made some prisoners feel better than being cooped up in their cells for long hours with only short trips into the exercise yard.

Just when they thought that spring was well and truly here, and at last it was getting warmer, a snowstorm arrived out of the blue, lasting only ten minutes, but doing the plants no good. Eric moaned. He said he'd have to keep the plants in the greenhouse longer than usual.

Without waking up, Annie shivered, thinking about snow, thinking how odd it was that their children had grown up without ever seeing snow at all while when they were young there was plenty for sledging, long winters when the snow seemed to be with them for weeks on end and wind which blew the snow into huge drifts. Annie recalled building an igloo in the garden with Sharon under instruction from her sister Barbara. They used a spade to cut the snow into large blocks which built up into the required shape. They made a tunnel to crawl in through. It was very hot inside and when they all began to breathe heavily, Barbara said there should be a hole in the roof to vent the room before they ran out of air. For all their efforts, the next morning all that remained of the igloo was a pile of snow.

Annie remembered a time when Mum, looking out of the window, could only see a small amount of snow on the ground, and hurried to get them ready for school. Then turning the corner with her older sister and Sharon they were confronted by a massive snow drift. Ready to go back home, Annie and Sharon reckoned without Barbara's determination. "Mum wants us to go to school and that's where we're going." She marched forward, the snow soon over-topping her Wellington boots. "Come on," she ordered, "This is fun."

Annie couldn't see any fun in it. Neither could Sharon. Tramping through the snow was hard work but it warmed them up. The first drift was small compared with the others they encountered on their journey to school. It occurred to Annie's drowsing brain that they could so easily have been buried in the deep snow that day. Then when they reached the school gates and the pathway being cleared by Mr Lumb, the caretaker, there was only one other boy who'd made it and a single teacher, Mrs Kirk, who lived across the road from the school. She ushered the four of them into the infants' classroom to seats by a roaring fire and gave them all hot milk warmed in a saucepan resting on a trivet by the fire. It occurred to Annie that huge fires were a normal feature in their homes then because most of the Dads worked in the mines and received a coal allowance as part of their wages.

At an early age, they learnt that fire was a dangerous thing, to be respected. They learnt to make spills for lighting fires, starting at the corner of a newspaper and rolling as tightly as possible to the opposite corner and then winding the paper, looping it into a knot so it would burn slowly and give the fire time to kindle. During the winter, fires would be banked up slack at night so that in the morning it wouldn't take long to rake the embers and rekindle the flames with a few spills and cobbles of coal.

The hardest chore was to carefully carry the ashes out to the dustbin; with the wind blowing hard the ash blew back into their faces, or worse still, into the kitchen where it was the devil to clear up the mess. Another hated job was to empty out the chamber pot they called a Po. They were commonplace in those days as the toilet was usually at the bottom of the garden.

Many fireplaces had an oven at the side and Annie remembered delicious stews heating when the fire was burning bright with hot embers and then when it cooled it needed mending. Mending for the uninitiated meant fetching a bucket of coal from the coalhouse situated behind the house, and then putting enough coal on so the fire would flare up again.

A girl in Annie's class at school called Josie said their fireplace had a boiler at the side where they got all their hot water. When they wanted a bath, they had a tin one which her Mum put out on the hearth every Friday night and then she would ladle in hot water so Josie and her five brothers and sisters could take it in turns to get bathed. Annie was pleased she had grown up with a bathroom, even though it was just a partitioned-off area at the end of the kitchen.

Annie's wandering thoughts brought her back into that snowy day in the infants' classroom. The four children took off their coats which the teacher hung up to dry while they drank their hot milk. Mrs Kirk made them take off their Wellington boots and she put their wet socks on the fireguard to dry them, along with their gloves, scarves and hats. It seemed a big adventure to them. When all the clothes were dry, the teacher got them all dressed again and told them to go straight home. Their journey back was much quicker as the snow ploughs had been out and cleared away the main drifts.

Annie and Barbara's Mum was surprised to see them and when she'd been out to see the snow for herself she said "Why didn't you come back?"

"You said we had to go to school," Annie's sister said with a grin.

"Cheeky monkey!" said her Mum. "Would you like some warm milk?"

"Can we have Cocoa, please?"

"Of course, you can, and while I'm making it you two can get out of those wet clothes and get yourselves into a hot bath. We don't want you catching a chill and missing school tomorrow."

The children groaned, but, of course, she was right.

10

Annie lay still, her young years and her beloved Eric fresh in her mind before she opened her eyes. When she finally did, she had no idea where she was, or why she was there.

"Do you need the toilet again, Annie?" a young woman asked.

"Where am I?"

"You're at the farm."

"I don't understand." Annie was getting agitated.

"I'm Lois," the girl with the dark plaits persisted, "Mary told me to watch for you to wake up and take you to the toilet, then a wash and some food." Lois put her strong arms around Annie and hoisted her to her feet. "Come along now. I have to do what Mary told me."

Still confused, Annie allowed herself to be led. Before long, she felt calmer since Lois had allowed her no argument as she went about her allotted tasks but was still struggling to overcome her weariness.

"Two spoonfuls and you can go back to bed." Annie tried hard to comply when the soup was offered up to her lips. "Very good," said Lois. "One more." It seemed a very long time since Annie had been spoken to like a small child, and she felt completely out of her depth and the fever had returned, making her shake uncontrollably so Lois helped her back onto her feet and guided her to her resting place.

"There." Lois gently tucked the sheepskins around Annie. "You'll remember everything soon Annie when the sickness goes. Just rest here and think about the good times."

Annie couldn't think what could have happened to bring her to this unfamiliar place. She couldn't understand why she was being looked after by children rather than friends or her beloved Eric. As she snuggled down into the warm fleece, she stopped shaking so much, but trying to recollect what had happened was too hard for her and she couldn't help dropping off again.

Her thoughts went way back to when the media was always reporting on Global Warming and people were saying it would be nice to be a little warmer anyway. They tended to take all these warnings lightly, because there always seemed to be something from the Government that they were supposed to be careful about.

Don't waste water when they had floods every year.

Don't eat eggs, and don't eat red meat and so far, nothing had happened, at least not in the epidemic proportions being predicted by the Government.

Annie remembered a newscaster saying Global Warming was getting out of hand, and they must be much more careful about recycling, and interviewing yet another scientist warning that the end of the world was nigh; saying that the melting of ice caps had slowed down after the volcanic eruptions in Iceland, spewing sulphur gas into the atmosphere, but over the last few years was escalating at a frightening rate; saying that the Boxing Day tsunami in the Philippines could occur in the southern part of the British Isles too because of the accelerated level of asteroids landing in the Atlantic Ocean; saying that the current scientific advice was falling on deaf ears.

"Another scaremonger, switch it off," snorted Eric but not long after he was shouting for Annie to come as quickly as possible. She rushed into the lounge, still drying her hands, to find him pointing at the television. "Look at that. They are talking about re-routing the Thames so it cascades over the cliffs of Dover to prevent the water rising and flooding half of London like it did last time. I can't believe they're going to re-route the Thames, can you?"

"I'm not really interested Eric," Annie said patiently. "My main concern at the moment is to get back in the kitchen and make sure I don't let my pies burn. Anyway, you know how this Government always handles everything, leaping from one crisis to another, without really considering the consequences."

Annie was half way back to her baking again when Eric shouted after her, "I think that it's a good idea. We don't want flooding in the Thames Valley again, do we? Look how many lives were lost the last time there were floods."

"So, what do you think they're going to do with the thousands of people who live where they're re-routing? Do you think, in your wildest dreams, they'll see it as an improvement? Not that it'll make any difference. Whatever the Government decide to do, they'll do."

Eric went back to the television and Annie could hear him periodically shouting at the broadcaster. They talked about it again over their evening meal, and on into the evening, but could not agree how to improve anything. As a last resort, Eric challenged Annie, "Well how would you solve the problem then?"

"I don't know, I'll go to bed and think about it," she retaliated sternly. She put down her knitting and headed for the door.

By the next week, the weather had improved greatly. It was even warm enough to go for a round of golf. Naturally the topic of conversation was the planned re-routing of the Thames. Paddy agreed with Eric that it was a good idea. Sharon agreed with Annie, that it had not been given enough thought. The debate continued throughout a game which was so enjoyable mainly because they had all been cooped up for so long and were all delighted to be out in the fresh air. No conclusion to the problem was reached when they said their goodbyes, agreeing to meet up again soon, if the good weather continued.

11

The people of the United Kingdom, and for that matter the world, were becoming increasingly frightened by the events taking place; more volcanoes erupting, causing massive devastation; a tsunami in Japan causing untold damage to the environment as it swamped a nuclear power station; further flooding in the British Isles was ravaging the countryside, fields under water for weeks and ground rendered unfit to grow crops for the foreseeable future, cows, sheep and horses cut off and drowned by the rising water, rescue impossible because of the relentless rain; earthquakes toppling skyscrapers. All the news seen on their television screens seemed bad.

Nearer home, their own rivers had become dark, deep, and unfriendly. The spring tide brought the bore up the River Severn, but few were expecting the ferocity of the water as it rose higher and higher, bursting the banks and indiscriminately drowning adventurous surfers riding it, and people watching from the banks.

Nature was taking control of the Earth and man could do very little about it.

Throughout the world, there was calamitous unrest. In the name of religion, bombs were set off killing hundreds. Disputes over which country owned which parcel of land were the cause of escalating fighting with many lives lost. Refugee numbers were increasing exponentially in camps waiting for different countries to take them in. There were hundreds of thousands of people fleeing their homelands because of the relentless violence.

The Thames burst its banks and this time, with huge loss of life. The Prime Minister on the television seemed helpless to offer even modest reassurance. "As you know," he said, "since Roman times, the City of London has encroached into the river, and building along the banks has thus made it narrower, deeper, and faster flowing. It is only a matter of time, before the rising tide, plus a sea surge or perhaps a tsunami, which is not beyond the realms of possibility according to the scientists who study this kind of thing, could conceivably cause more massive flooding perhaps even worse than we have just witnessed. This loss of life is unacceptable but we did not expect the Thames Barrier to fail for some years yet. Evidently, their calculations were incorrect and we as a Government, have to stop another catastrophe occurring and, therefore, we have decided to go ahead with the plans to re-route the river."

Within days of the speech, there were protests in the streets, some of them violent. It was noticeable that when next interviewed, the Prime Minister looked drawn and careworn, his hair beginning to grey at the temples, and obviously under enormous pressure. This time, the interviewer was the ever-popular Jerry Stone, a thin-faced, bearded man, with yellowing teeth, and receding fair hair worn in an archaic ponytail. He wore brightly coloured clothes and adopted a controversial approach to all his interviews and no exception would be made for the Prime Minister.

Taking once more the stance that his Government had been discussing the Thames re-routing programme for the last six months and had determined this is to be the best way forward to ensure the safety of the Thames Valley, the Prime Minister found himself on the receiving end of considerable sarcasm. Jerry Stone questioned the obvious flaw in re-routing any river. "Do you think that there's been enough discussion with the people you're planning to uproot with this scheme?"

"Yes. Instead of going around in circles, we're pressing ahead because this is the safest and best option. As your Government, we have to have the courage to take even unpopular decisions."

"So, how much is this going to cost the taxpayer?"

The Prime Minister quickly moved to say how this was going to help people rather than answering Jerry Stone's question. "And the scheme will provide work for the foreseeable future. That cannot be a bad thing, can it?"

The question of cost was pressed again and again avoided so Jerry Stone asked "How are people going to be compensated for loss of their property?"

The Prime Minister's answer was that they would all be better off being moved now rather than being drowned later. "Let's put this in perspective. The scientists have confirmed that the ice cap will be de-stabilised and moving south within the next two years. As I have explained to you many times before, we don't intend to wait until this disaster is reality."

"Could you be wrong putting your trust in scientists?"

"Would you like to be the one who took that risk?" countered the Prime Minister. He stood, collecting his papers from the table.

The debate was over.

12

Spring days turned to summer and most people had begun to accept that what was occurring had probably been for the best. Work had begun in earnest. Great walls were being constructed at the mouth of the Thames and further along the coastline to present an impenetrable barrier for the river waters flowing along on their new intended course.

There was considerable protest though. Thousands began marching and waving banners over the forced exodus of people from *the green route,* protests which often ended in violence as tensions were running high, and many people didn't accept the inevitable enormity of what would happen if the programme was suspended. The country was in chaos. The army had been called in to help the police keep out saboteurs trying to destroy the machines digging out the new river channel. Progress was slower than anticipated in the hottest summer on record with record numbers dying from the intense heat, not just the elderly but young children too. There was no respite from the heat and shops soon ran out of supplies of fans adding fuel to the idea that Global Warming had begun in earnest. Crops were failing and famine was rife in some parts of the world. A great cloud of doom loomed, and not just in the Thames Valley.

Annie and Eric's personal lives continued to revolve around plans for their Golden Wedding party next summer if national affairs didn't frustrate things. There were still protests going on, but they lost momentum as the work progressed. The summer heat was intense and they needed rain. "Careful what you wish for," was the comment from a long-range weather forecaster predicting rain for the whole of June. He was right too. It was the wettest June on record. By the end of the month everyone was depressed by the constant rain, but if anything, the intensity of an exceptionally hot July and August proved even worse than the continuous rain had as it was impossible to get out due to the intensity of the heat. Even September, with cooler temperatures, was the hottest September on record.

Eric had protected most of his plants from the heat and had managed to reap a great harvest. He had even managed to grow a few lemons. "These are great!" Annie exclaimed, taking them from him, "But hurry up and get your boots off. There's some interesting news on the television."

"What's happened?" asked an exasperated Eric, pulling off his gardening boots in time to hear an excited newscaster talking about the Thames which had begun to flow in the new direction that day. The cameras switched to the opening of the sluice gates. There was euphoria in the crowds gathered to watch the event as the waters began flowing down their new course. The cheering, clapping, shouting and whistling went on for some time. The scene moved from one view to another as the excitement grew with the release of more and more water through the sluices. The route was lined with thousands of people all wanting to witness this phenomenon. It would be an event talked about for years to come. *Where were you when the Thames cascaded into the sea?*

The world media was on hand to transmit around the globe. Other countries had shown interest in changing the course of their own rivers to try to stop flooding of their low-lying regions. It took several hours for the water to reach its destination but at last, the water cascaded into the sea. It was a magnificent sight and one the Prime Minister exploited ruthlessly, telling everyone that the people of the Thames Valley would now be safe from flooding when the inevitable happened and sea levels rose. He said that flooding could never happen again.

Eric said, "Look at him, milking it for all he's worth."

Annie and Eric were still planning another trip to Australia to see John, Amanda and Melanie and her husband Jay's new baby boy, Callum. Annie had been busy over the last few months knitting Callum jumpers and cardigans to take with them. She was making them bigger ready for next winter as it would be the height of their summer when they got there. It had been six years since the last visit but they wanted to include travelling the extra two thousand miles to see Stuart who now owned his own sheep-station.

Of all their grandchildren, Stuart was the most like Eric, not physically but in other ways. He was a serious man and it was a rarity to see him really laugh but he could be a joker, although sometimes his humour was a bit weird, and took a bit of getting used to. Somehow though, Eric was on the same wave-length.

Their flights hadn't yet been booked; they were waiting until nearer the date just in case they couldn't make it and wouldn't be able to get a refund. John phoned them to check they weren't delaying for health reasons, assuring them that if they booked now and became ill before the flight they could get a full refund from the insurance company.

"No worries," Annie told him. "We still want to leave it until the last minute before booking. The money may as well stay in our bank rather than theirs," she laughed.

"Have you seen the new route of the Thames on your news?" enquired Eric when Annie passed the phone across to him. John replied that he thought that it was all very exciting. He wanted to know if they had watched it on television as it cascaded into the English Channel. They talked about the event for some time before it was time to say goodbye.

The excitement of the river flowing over the cliffs soon became old news. With the heat-wave, it didn't take long for the old river bed to dry out. The centre was still a little muddy, but different groups of people decided to walk from one side to the other despite notices warning that this could be dangerous. This continued for a while until the surveyors declared that the bed was dry and ready for stage two, its re-development. Apparently, the Government had decided many months before to throw the plans open to all architects in the United Kingdom. "We want to make this the best design ever." They meant *without having to put the contracts out abroad*. "We want our country to lead the world in innovative design." They had allowed four months for plans to be submitted and a further two months to narrow it down to ten designs. These would then be eliminated by telephone and text voting, much like the competitions which had been all the rage on the television over the last few years. The idea with the most votes would win the contract. This process had been taking place while the river was being diverted. Thousands of houses were going to be built, with sports facilities, shops, restaurants, and libraries. The building area would extend from the Isis to the old mouth of the Thames, now blocked off from the sea with the latest technology, the finest sea wall in the world. The engineering teams, who had designed it, assured the public that never again would London be flooded.

The chief engineer, a man named Adrian Bradley, interviewed on television, said he was extremely confident they now had the answer to all the design faults of the original Thames Barrier. Bradley fielded all manner of technical questions but one remark seemed a bit odd. He said that after he had personally examined the point at which the diversion was to commence, it had occurred to him that this had not been the natural flow of the Thames and he believed that an explosion had made it flow in the direction they had all been used to it travelling. When asked what he meant by this remark he simply stated as his belief that "The river hasn't always flowed through London; probably centuries ago it travelled south."

The reporters jostled around him. "Can you prove it?" someone shouted. Bradley simply answered that it was only his opinion backed by forty years' engineering expertise.

Annie, shaking now, was battling a fever which was threatening her life. Mary gave her a drink made by crushing poppy seeds with other herbs to help her sleep soundly, instead of fitfully as she had been.

13

Machinery moved in to remove the top soil from the river. This was excellent for growing and the public was led to believe that farmers wanted it for spreading on fields which had been flooded. None were sure this was true, but nevertheless, it was dug up and loaded onto fleets of lorries to be taken away. The excavation had been continuing for a while when one of the workmen stopped and climbed down from his cab to investigate something solid the bucket had come up against. Carefully, he used a spade to move some of the debris so he could get a better look. It appeared to be stone. He shrugged before getting back into his machine and expertly removing more of the soil. The ground was firm now as the hot sun had dried out all the mud. The stone was gradually uncovered as the digger removed more soil and when the edges of it were showing the stone was revealed to measure about the size of a large door. The workman, a stocky

Londoner called Joe Franks, thought it interesting enough to stop work and radio for his boss to come and have a look.

The foreman was a tall, strong man in his early forties. He was clean-shaven and his curly dark hair was covered by his yellow hard-hat. Laughter lines abounded on his suntanned face especially around his eyes which seemed to be laughing all the time. He wouldn't stand for any nonsense from his men, especially if he thought that they were skiving but he had worked with Joe for a number of years – in fact, Joe had taught him a lot about the building trade when he was a youngster starting work and Richard Soames liked Joe and respected his opinion. If Joe thought something was worth investigating then it probably was.

Richard stood beside Joe looking at the slab of stone. "Any idea what it could be?"

"Beats me." In all my years I've never seen anything like it."

Richard bent down and rubbed his rough, work-hardened hand over the stone. He cleared away some of the clay covering a dent in the stone near the top of the longest side, revealing a metal bar.

"Looks to be some kind of handle." Richard got hold of the metal and snapped back from it. "Bloody Hell." He began rubbing his fingers. "I swear it gave me an electric shock Joe."

"Can't be," retorted Joe. "It's been under water for donkey's years."

"You feel it then," said Richard. "What kind of metal can be under water and remain in such good condition?"

Joe chuckled, reaching down to feel the metal bar and jumping back immediately. "Sod! I got a shock too."

The two men stood for a while looking at each other. Then Joe said, "Should I put a chain on and see if it'll lift?"

"Yeah! We could try. But don't hold your breath. I'm not sure we should be using a chain if it's giving off an electric shock."

The men fastened a chain to Joe's machine but when they tried to connect it to the bar, sparks flew in all directions, and after several attempts, they gave up.

"That's it then. We'll just have to pass this on to a higher authority. I don't want to be responsible for this. Just put some of those orange and white tapes around it to keep anyone off, Joe, and I'll see if I can get Mr Philips to come and take a look."

The next day, Philips came with two other men, all three wearing suits and ties, green Wellington boots, and white hard-hats. Apart from their headgear they looked out of place on the building site. Philips looked down at the stone slab and rubbed his chin. "What seems to be the problem then?" He was addressing Richard.

"Well," said Richard, "we aren't sure how to move it, or if it needs moving at all."

"We have checked the oldest plans we have to hand," said the second of the men. He was very thin and kept rubbing his hands together as if he was cold. "We can't find any trace of anything at all in this area, sir. There are no plans for sewage or anything which could possibly need to be covered by a slab."

The third man, who was much younger than the others, fresh faced with the eager expression of youth said, "Do you think Adrian Bradley could have been right then and the river's not always covered this land? What do you think, Frank?"

Frank stopped rubbing his hands and started to nod in agreement.

"What are you talking about?" spluttered Mr Philips, mopping the bald patch over his forehead with a pristine handkerchief. Then he took off his round designer glasses and started to clean them. Ignoring the younger men, he said, "You do realise that we're behind schedule."

At this point, since no decision seemed forthcoming, Richard took control, suggesting they thread some rope under the metal bar and attempt to move the stone. He already knew that chain was no good as it conducted electricity. "The only other alternative is to smash it up."

Mr Philips mopped his brow some more and said "Get Joe into his cab and see if he can smash up the stone." For some reason, he didn't just say it directly to Joe.

Joe Franks walked to his machine, climbed into the cab and brought the bucket down with a crash into the centre of the stone.

Everybody was standing well back to ensure they couldn't be hit by splinters of rock but they were all stunned when the bucket shattered into a pile of mangled metal pieces.

Joe couldn't believe his eyes. "What're we going to do now?" he shouted, "An' who's gonna pay to replace my bucket?"

The two younger men looked at each other but said nothing. An agitated Mr Philips mopped his brow, and then removed his glasses to rub them with his handkerchief, completely ignoring Joe. Richard scratched his head after removing his hard-hat for a moment and said, "Shall we try the rope then?"

Joe had already climbed down. "What about 'lectric shock then?" he muttered.

By now, Mr Philips was red faced and sweating with anxiety. "Electric shock! What on Earth is this man talking about?" He turned from one to the other expecting some response that wasn't forthcoming.

Joe certainly didn't feel obliged to explain how he and Richard had received a shock from the metal handle. The fresh-faced young man put his hand up with his first finger pointing to the sky, as a pupil might to his teacher.

"Well, Brendan," scowled Philips.

"I told you in your office, sir. That metal bar gives off an electric shock. Mr Soames and Mr Franks both got a shock from it yesterday, as I told you." He repeated himself nervously.

Mr Philips just snorted in disapproval.

Richard fastened a length of thick rope around a metal hook attached to Joe's machine. Grunting with the effort, he gingerly threaded the other end through the gap under the bar on the stone, making sure his fingers didn't come into contact with the metal.

"There now Joe, try that." Richard spoke in his usual friendly manner.

Joe, back in his cab, worked the necessary levers. The rope tightened to the point where it looked as though it would snap. Richard ushered the three men further back as a precaution. The slab moved slightly. Joe stopped his machine for a second and before he could start it up again, and to the surprise of all the men, the great stone slab lifted up into the air by itself, like a huge door. The hinges were spring loaded and looked in excellent condition.

Mr Philips, Brendan and Frank edged nearer to the large opening, carefully keeping behind Richard who sprang back into them as though he'd been shot. Recovering his composure, he ushered them all to a safer distance. "It's the smell."

Joe joined them, holding his arm across his nose and mouth and his eyes were streaming. "The stench down there – like someone died." The smell was so strong now that none of them could go nearer without their eyes running and a feeling of nausea.

Philips announced that he and his two companions were going back to the office to make a few phone calls and get advice on what to do next. "We'll be back tomorrow," he called over his shoulder as the three of them made their way off-site. As an afterthought, he added "Richard, I'm relying on you to sort things out here."

Joe and Richard then searched the area for some thick pieces of suitable wood. Between them, they carried a couple of sturdy planks over to the hole, holding their breath as they strategically positioned them to stop the door closing completely so the smell could dissipate overnight. Joe went back to his cab and expertly lowered the stone door. There were creaks and groans when it came to rest on the planks but somehow the wood held. Then Joe disengaged his machine so no one could move it. Finally they put the orange and white tape around both the machine and the stone slab.

"That's a job well done!" Joe declared in a matter of fact manner as though it had just been a regular day's work.

Richard slapped him on the back. "We may as well stop work now and come back to this in the morning."

As they walked away Joe laughed and said, "I don't think I've ever been up and down into that cab so much as I have today."

The two men walked amiably from the building site. "Don't worry about replacing the bucket," said Richard. "I'll see the company buys a new one."

14

By seven thirty the next morning they were both back on site and two strangers were walking purposefully toward them. The oldest, a man in his fifties, shook hands first with a smile. He had obviously been used to hard work in his time; his large hands still bore the calluses. As he was shaking hands, he introduced himself. "I'm Les Smith and I'm a mining engineer. This is my assistant."

"Martin Armstrong." He in his turn shook hands. Like his boss he had short cropped hair, was tall, clean-shaven and had the same air of confidence about him. Both men set down rucksacks containing obviously heavy equipment.

Richard and Joe stood back and watched as they laid things out in an orderly fashion.

Les said to Richard, "Let's have a look at this stone of yours then."

"Hope it smells better than yesterday. It was horrendous. Couldn't get near enough to look down the hole."

Martin put his testing meter near the opening and lifted it up to see what it was registering. "I think we can raise the stone now, Joe. If that's okay with you?"

"Fine by me," said Joe. As he strode off to his machine he thought to himself, *what a difference to Mr Bloody Philips yesterday.*

"Best stand back," suggested Richard.

Joe started up his engine. The rope creaked and groaned and then the stone lifted by itself to the amazement of the newcomers.

"Wow!" said Les.

"Jeeze!" That was Martin.

They all stared up at the stone for a second or two before walking forward. Les was the first one to the brink of the hole. He peered into the depths and said, "Would you believe it, there are steps here." He sounded excited.

Martin had brought over a lamp, not unlike the Davey Lamp used by coal miners years ago to test for gas. He went down a few steps, cautiously. As his yellow hard-hat disappeared, Les called out to him but Martin was coming back up by then, smiling from ear to ear "Absolutely no sign of gas. In fact the air down there is pretty fresh and breathable."

Martin returned to their laid-out equipment and brought back other types of meter and a torch for each of them.

"Does that mean we can have a look down there?" Joe said hopefully, as he turned the torch around in his hands.

"Course you can. That's why I've brought you a torch."

Les grinned and said, "You didn't think we were going to leave intrepid explorers on the surface did you? I would suggest we use two of the torches and keep the other two in reserve, just in case."

Martin hoisted his rucksack over one shoulder and followed Les down the steps. Tentatively Richard followed with Joe bringing up the rear. Surprisingly, the steps were all exactly the same; no wear and tear, no dips in the centre from feet eroding the stone over the years as in old castle staircases. The torches cast eerie shadows as they were shone up and down while the party stopped to allow Martin to gather samples from the walls.

"Hey, Les. Look at this."

"Problem?" said Les.

"Only problem is I can't get any of the stone to scrape away. It's almost not like stone at all. If I didn't know better I'd say this could be some kind of material I've never seen before."

"Interesting," was the only comment from Les. They stood for a moment and then Les made a decision. "Right, let's get to the bottom of these steps first, Martin, and we can worry about that later."

"But I'm unable to take any samples and that's what I'm supposed to be doing."

"Time is getting on, Martin," said Les, "and we must at least know what's down here."

"You're the boss." Martin shrugged.

They made better progress after that because they weren't constantly stopping every few steps for Martin to scrape the rock or whatever it was.

"Eureka!" shouted Les. "We're at the bottom."

He waited for the other three to catch up. When they did, Richard switched on his torch and shone it up to the ceiling and then around the cavern.

"How exciting is this?" exclaimed Martin, leaping around like an overgrown school boy when he came across a passageway. Joe had found a second one leading off to the left, and Les was standing inside a third leading straight on.

"Come on," said Les. Throwing caution to the wind, he set off at some pace. The others followed in hot pursuit until Les called out over his shoulder to be careful of any potholes in the cave floor. Suddenly Les stopped stock still and the others almost bumped into him. "Look." Les shone his torch on two stone statues like Egyptian guards from the tomb of Tutankhamen.

The tall figures held spears over a doorway. Below the crossed spears was an inscription in an unrecognisable language. Martin used his mobile phone to take photographs. Les had a proper camera and took a close-up of the writing. "Is this some kind of warning?" He was only saying aloud what the others were thinking. It didn't stop him having the foresight to take another photograph, this time of Joe and Richard standing in front of the stone guards.

"We better go back now and report in. This looks like a job for the archaeologists."

Richard said, "You're in charge." His reluctance to leave with further discoveries to be made was obvious in his voice.

On the surface, work progressed across the rest of the building site, while the powers that be debated what to do about the vast underground chambers Les and the others had found. It seemed sensible to keep news of the discovery of the steps away from the media as long as possible, not least to avoid disrupting the hundreds of workers toiling away giving the much-heralded economic boost promised by the Prime Minister.

Fortunately, media attention was heavily focused on yet another African famine and floods in South America. Reporters clustered to cover the relief measures being taken by various countries including the provision of newly prefabricated houses, part of an unusually speedily co-ordinated international governmental effort rather than leaving aid work to charities.

World events gave the Thames discovery a breathing space but the lack of any sense of urgency to gather specialist exploratory teams meant that when the news of the steps eventually leaked, there was media frenzy. Everyone wanted to know what was down there. The stories of ancient monsters or an alien race became wilder by the hour simply because there were no authoritative answers, just a mystery still to be uncovered.

Finally, a Government spokesman came on television admitting that proper underground inspections had not yet taken place but that he would personally ensure the public were informed of any discoveries made. It was too little, too late and did nothing to quell media interest or the potent mix of public fascination and alarm. News of the discovery of the steps spread like global wildfire, and everyone wanted to know what was down there being guarded by barriers and armed police officers.

A chief archaeologist, Professor James of the British Museum, had already been appointed and his first move had been to distribute copies of the photographs Les had taken to colleagues around the world to see if any of them could understand the inscription which was definitely not Egyptian Sumerian, Chinese, Coptic, Celtic or even Aztec.

Professor James' move backfired when the press got hold of the photographs fuelling renewed media speculation. The photographs made the front page of almost every newspaper in the world. The official response, that it was of prime importance the message was understood before the door could be opened, was less well covered.

The next morning there were crowds of people on the building site and police reinforcements had to be called in to hold back the onlookers so that a team of eminent archaeologists could get through. They were an international bunch drawn from different museums across the world, but most of them shared a common conviction that the statues must be of Egyptian origin.

A large procession of men and women went down the steps and then split into three groups so that each of the separate passages could be investigated. The first group who went to the left did not have to travel far before coming to a stone door. It was not difficult to open as the leader of the group, Guy Adams, had worked on the pyramids so the knack to opening the door involved familiar processes he had seen before. The opening allowed a horrific stench to escape but oddly it didn't take long to dissipate and be replaced by breathable air.

This time the team was fully prepared and immediately set up proper lighting enabling them to view an amazing sight. Stacked neatly along the walls were shelves upon shelves of artefacts, golden goblets and trays, combs for the hair, and fans, pots of every size and description, and jewellery of every design imaginable, many decorated with precious stones, some of a type never been seen before.

The explorers looked around in awe. They saw statues both large and small, with the most intricate carving and paintings stacked carefully along a side wall protected with some kind of material in between each canvas so that not one was touching another.

Adams, a sturdy man with a shock of grey hair, a well-lined face with sad brown eyes, and the soft hands of an office worker, took a laptop out of his bag and instructed his team that everything be registered and photographed. He told them that in all his time in the Middle East, he had never been privy to such a discovery, and they must record everything carefully.

"We'll have to see about transporting the whole lot to the surface, and that requires crates for each artefact once it's been photographed and catalogued," he said before setting each member of the team the task of making a note of everything in their allocated section of the cave. He also set up a camera crew to take photographs of every single item, no matter how small.

On a pedestal, close to the door was a small but beautiful marble female statue with her arms raised to hold a large, intricately decorated ewer on her shoulder. Adams lifted it from the column on which it stood to admire the exquisite workmanship. Immediately when he lifted it he was shocked to see a vaporised gas beginning to pour into the room. As he started to choke on the fumes he yelled for everyone to evacuate as fast as possible.

Men and women hurried to obey, their eyes streaming and many of them gasping for air. When the last person had vacated the chamber, the door simply closed by itself and huge stones slid into place effectively sealing the room from further disturbance.

Adams insisted on a roll call to make sure everybody was out and safe. Coughing and spluttering, the staff stated their names and headed up the steps so first aid could be given to the ones who were finding it difficult to breathe.

Adams himself stayed to check the sealed doorway. The slabs looked like stone but in his heart Adams knew already that they weren't made of any material with which he was familiar or knew how to cut.

15

The passageway to the right led to a door which seemed impossible to open.

Marion Dewsbury was a pale-faced woman in her mid-sixties, dressed, as always, in trousers and an old shirt, worn to disguise her ample body. She had brogues on her feet and walked in a duck-like fashion. She seemed an unlikely candidate to be leading an expedition into the depths of the tomb, but she was an expert in her field who had been personally selected by Professor James, who had known and respected her for years. Knowing of her terminal cancer, he was keen to make her last professional tasks noteworthy.

"Now Marion," he said in a fatherly manner, "you'll stop if it becomes too much for you."

"Of course," she assured him. She loved her work and would keep going as long as she possibly could.

Among the others in Marion's party was a clever young man, fresh out of university. He had short dark hair with shining milky grey eyes, the sinewy build of youth, and, the reason Marion was so pleased to have him, he showed pure commitment to the job. His name was Philip, although everyone except his Mum called him Phil. He had gained his degree in computer technology with honours before obtaining his Master's in Archaeology.

Opening the door in question had seemed less straightforward than that facing Mr Adams' team and they decided to drill through it. It proved hard work. They constantly had to replace drill bits because the qualities of the stone were unlike any other the men had encountered before. They took it in turns to drill as arms quickly tired. After many attempts and a goodly number of broken drill bits they had scarcely scratched the surface and had to admit defeat.

Over an hour later, while most of the team were standing around scratching their heads, the door suddenly opened seemingly of its own accord. Simultaneously Phil shouted "Eureka," very loudly from further down the passageway. He had found a small metal ring set almost hidden in the wall of the passageway. He could only get one finger into it but when he tugged on the ring the mighty door swung wide. It didn't seem a coincidence.

Again this team was forced to retreat for a period while the smell from the closed room dissipated but eventually after testing the air quality they could set up lights and see what they'd found.

The harshly lit cavern contained shelves fully stacked with items but to their anguished surprise whenever an object was handled it simply disintegrated and fell to the floor as a pile of dust.

"So, what do we do now?" one of them asked a crest-fallen Marion.

"I don't know."

Phil had in the meantime picked up a contraption which looked like a child's Game Boy. He pressed a few buttons and while it didn't disintegrate neither did it do anything.

"Should you do that?" someone said but it was too late and Phil had prised the back plate off the unit with the end of a screwdriver. Phil was oblivious to everything else and continued poking inside the device. "Ah!" he said after a time. Then he took a small battery-powered soldering iron out of his rucksack and began to tackle some loose wiring. Other members of the group gathered around with interest as Phil worked. Let's see what happens now." Phil was speaking for his own benefit. He pressed one of the buttons on the toy and, from the opposite side of the cave to where the shelves were, there was movement and a creaking noise.

Everyone turned in the direction of the noise. Phil pressed the other button which to him was patently obviously the off button. He grinned at the rest of the group as he held up the console. "Just needs slight adjustment." He again removed the back and did something with a tiny jeweller's screwdriver. Then he put it all back together and tried once more.

This time, there was no creaking noise, just the emitted light as a hologram of a man appeared. Shocked, everyone stood perfectly still; everyone except Phil. He walked over to stand unflinching in front of the figure as the hologram lifted an arm, something resembling a gun in his hand. The team held its collective breath spellbound as Phil spoke quietly to the projection asking who he was.

The figure looked down at the gun-like object and pressed a small button. "This is a translator." The voice had a metallic edge to it but was perfectly understandable. "It can speak any language and enables me to converse with you."

The others relaxed and moved forward a little with Marion now beside Phil introducing herself and then her colleague as though addressing an actual person.

The hologram spoke in turn. "My name is Dr Black and I am charged with ensuring that you do not have Ceasuritathalon. If you would form a line, I will take you one at a time."

The room was abuzz with conversation. The questions on most lips were what he meant by *Ceasur-whatever* and why any of them would have it? Marion suggested they do as requested, and amid much chattering, everyone took their place in the queue.

Dr Black started with Phil. He swept a handheld instrument over him from top to toe and then waved him over to the right. Marion was second and Dr Black gestured her to his left. She did as he asked and stood watching fascinated. Most members of the group were dismissed to join Phil, leaving another man of about her own age and a younger woman standing with Marion.

Next, Dr Black pressed other buttons on his hand-held console and passed it slowly and carefully over Marion. Then he dismissed her in the manner of a teacher to his pupil and turned to the man.

"I'm not supposed to be here. I should have been trying to decode the message Mr Adams was focussing on. But I thought I'd stick with my friend, Marion."

"It won't hurt," said the hologram.

Marion could see the anxiety in the balding, overweight maths genius with the thick bottle-top glasses. "It's fine, Harry," she reassured him. "Let him do what he needs to."

Harry tried to smile. He had known Marion and her late husband for so many years, he trusted her judgement implicitly. He turned back to Dr Black. "Okay," he said.

Marion switched her attention back to Phil who was holding what appeared to be a rucksack made from a light material which looked like tinfoil, but there was no way it could be or it would have torn as he picked it up.

"It feels warm to the touch."

Another man, an American called Noel, asked Phil if he could hold it. Noel was about the same age as Phil, and an expert in the same field. He had graduated in America and his wealthy parents had financed him to go with an expedition which was trying to find Noah's Ark, a project abandoned because of civil unrest in and around Egypt. When news of tombs in England broke, Noel was desperate to be involved and got his parents to part-finance the exploration to ensure he could be in on it. "What gave you the idea of fixing the wiring to make the hologram come alive, Phil?"

The answer, couched in technical details, proved to Noel that he'd found a kindred spirit even though they were complete opposites in terms of physical appearance. Noel was a far better fit than Phil for the pasty-faced, overweight stereotype of the computer nerd. Together they carefully examined the rucksack, opening the fastening to find it contained something like a metal box. They agreed that the lack of weight to it meant it could not be any metal known to man. On the underside of the rucksack, Noel came across another flap, this one containing a small handset with four buttons set around a central point. Intrigued, he pressed a button but nothing happened. He pressed the others in turn. Still nothing.

"You'll probably have to work your magic on these controls too, Phil."

"Probably best to take it back to the office for further investigation."

"Agreed."

The other member of the team who had been kept to one side by Dr Black was a young woman who had worked with Marion for a few years since she leaving school. Sarah was unaware that she owed her job to her Grandfather's direct approach to Marion, who he'd asked to give her the chance others had not in view of the difficulties caused by her severe Rheumatoid Arthritis. Professor James' only granddaughter possessed sharp features, hair scraped back into a French Twist and a mouth seemly set in a permanent scowl. Her bony fingers seemed to be twisted and she walked in an odd manner as though every step was painful.

Dr Black ran his device over Sarah from top to toe. Not knowing quite why, she found herself smiling at the doctor, just as she'd noticed Marion had earlier. Dismissed, as she turned to go Sarah noticed another console sitting on a low ledge. It looked much like the one Phil had discovered so she picked it up to show him. "Look, I know nothing about the technical side of computers. I'm just here to make notes for Marion but is this like the other one? I found it over there." She pointed across to the ledge.

Phil gently took the machine from her hands. Sarah spoke again, hardly pausing for breath. "My name's Sarah and I'm over the moon – well, not literally but you know what I mean – because Marion allowed me to come down here. She usually dictates everything and then I type it up for her, but this time..."

Phil held up a hand to stop her before she could say any more. He had no intention of allowing her to make herself seem foolish for gabbling on. He assumed it was because she was excited and nervous and was sublimely unaware of the attraction she felt towards him.

"Well done," he said calmly. Let's look at your find."

A smirking Noel came over to look too. Phil pressed the equivalent button on this device. Again, there were creaking and groaning sounds but nothing else. He tried again.

"I don't think it's going to work, do you?" Sarah spluttered with her words, thrilled to be involved so closely with Phil.

"Patience!" said Noel.

Phil tried once more and another holographic male figure appeared. The hologram waved his arms in the air, moved his mouth in an agitated manner, and then was gone.

"I'm afraid the water may have damaged the controls," said Phil. "If you look at the roof of the cave," he pointed to the ceiling above them, and everyone looked upwards, "you can see where water's been getting in. Only one tiny globule at a time, but it's been happening for a vast number of years and has caused all this damage. It's why we have putrefied and decomposed materials here." He swung his arm out in an arc over the heaps of ravaged artefacts.

"I think that you're probably right," agreed Noel as tiny particles began falling away from the console.

The cave was huge and as no one had found anything else intact, Marion decided they would take the rucksack and the two consoles to the surface. Everyone was sad that their finds had been less satisfying than they would have liked but there was nothing to be done about that. Noel carried the rucksack and behind him Phil brought the only other find, the two consoles.

The hologram's voice called after them. "You may not remove my console or it will self-destruct." Phil stopped short of the doorway and Marion reached his side. "What should I do, boss?"

Dr Black repeated, "You may not remove my console or it will self-destruct."

Phil and Marion looked at each other and then she took the consoles out of Phil's hands and returned them to where they'd been found.

Then both headed for the door.

Back at the surface, they were greeted by hordes of people, shouting and cheering, and also multiple flashes from cameras, as reporters jostled to get answers from the emerging archaeologists.

Marion immediately took charge. "My name is Professor Marion Dewsbury. It is with great sadness, I have to report that because of water damage sustained over centuries, we have made no major discoveries." She had no intention of giving out any information at this stage until she knew what they were dealing with.

One of the reporters called out "Didn't you find anything at all, Professor?"

Marion walked briskly away towards their police escort saying "That is all ladies and gentlemen."

There was a concerted groan from the crowd. Many people had waited all day to be on the scene hoping to see treasures brought up from the cave. The police began to disperse the thousands upon thousands of assembled bystanders. It was going to be a long night.

16

The next day Marion had an appointment to see her oncologist. Her last scan had resulted in a hopeless prognosis. She had left Phil and Noel in her office with instructions to see what they could do with the rucksack and arranged to meet them for a late lunch in a nearby restaurant. "My treat," she told them as she closed the door and left for the hospital.

This time Marion had a complete body scan. The nurses with her had met her many times over the last year. They were very professional and efficient. When the scan was over, one of them escorted her to the oncologist's office. The oncologist was an elderly man with that peculiarly steely kindness typical of certain surgeons. When she entered the room, he looked up and smiled, asking her to take a seat. Marion sat opposite him and waited as he looked at the images on his screen. After a few moments he said, "I've never seen anything like it before Mrs Dewsbury."

Marion sank down further into her chair expecting the worst.

The doctor looked at her and began again, quickly this time as he was not in the business of causing unnecessary distress.

"Mrs Dewsbury, the cancer has completely gone," he declared. "I don't understand it at all. I've compared today's scan with last week's and there is absolutely no sign whatsoever of a growth. Of course, we would like to run further tests, but you seem to be completely free from cancer."

Marion smiled with shocked relief. She stood and shook hands with the doctor before quietly leaving him shaking his head in disbelief at the computer screen showing her body scan. As she left the hospital heading for the car, Marion almost felt like skipping. Her smile had now set in a big grin which spread almost from ear to ear.

The two young men were waiting for her at the restaurant. They were astonished when she told them her news. Both were asking how this could have happened. The waitress came for their order and as they ate lunch Marion's euphoria radiated. Noel said, "How are we going to celebrate?"

"First things first," said Marion conspiratorially, touching her forefinger to her nose.

Back at her office Marion immediately picked up the telephone and dialled. "Hello," was all she said.

"Hi Marion," Harry replied. Marion said nothing. "Are you still there Marion?"

"Sure," she said, "do you have anything to tell me?"

"Yes, I do. Something very strange has occurred today. I woke up this morning and reached for my glasses from the bedside table, but when I put them on I couldn't see a damn thing. My first thought was that it was going to cost me another three hundred pounds for new ones."

"You always were tight when it came to spending money," Marion chuckled, "but do go on."

"Well, this is where it gets very strange. I went to the bathroom to get my medicine from the cabinet. You know I've got emphysema don't you?"

"I do," Marion said, beginning to become irritated. "Just get on with it Harry."

"As I said, I couldn't see in my glasses, so I didn't bother putting them on when I went to the bathroom. Then to my amazement, I could read all the writing on the tablet boxes. So I took the paper from inside, you know the one I mean, telling you all about side effects and I could read every word, even the name of the printer at the bottom of the sheet. But Marion, what do you think about my talking, can you tell I'm not gasping for breath every few words?"

"Sorry to trump that, Harry, but I don't have cancer anymore." Marion's bombshell made Harry gasp as he sucked in his breath. The silence was palpable. Marion broke it by telling Harry about her visit to the hospital.

Neither could rationally explain what had happened until something occurred to Harry. "What about the hologram, Dr Black?"

"I was thinking along those lines," agreed Marion. "Could you meet me for dinner tonight and we can decide what to do next?"

No sooner had Marion replaced the telephone than Sarah burst into the room. She couldn't stop for breath when she spoke normally, but today, she was so agitated that words were coming from her mouth so quickly that she was making no sense whatsoever. Phil and Nocl came in after her to see what all the fuss was about.

Marion spoke firmly to her, ordering her to sit down. Sarah complied but couldn't keep still, waving her hands about under Marion's nose. "It's gone, can you see, it's gone?"

"What has?" asked Noel.

Marion put her arm around Sarah to calm her. Sarah started to cry. Tears flowed down her cheeks and she shook with emotion as Marion patted her shoulder gently saying, "Rheumatoid Arthritis is a very painful ailment Sarah, but now you're cured, just as I've been cured of cancer."

Sarah stopped crying and wiped her eyes with her hand. Her big watery blue eyes peered up at her boss. "You're cured?" Marion nodded. "And Harry?" Sarah implored.

Again Marion nodded.

Realisation spread over Sarah's face and instead of her usual scowl her lips shaped into an amazing smile which lit up her whole being. "The pain's gone," she explained to the two young men who were astounded at the change in her appearance.

Phil said it for both of them. "Your face...you look beautiful." Neither could take their eyes from her. She looked years younger than they had previously thought her to be. The Ugly Duckling had emerged as a beautiful Swan.

Phil reached out to hold Sarah's hand, as he said to Marion, "What are we going to do about this?"

"You three are going to do nothing. Not a word to anyone. Do you understand?"

All three indicated their reluctant acceptance.

"I'm meeting Harry tonight so we can decide what to do. We don't want a riot on our hands do we."

Just then the sun broke out from behind the clouds which until that moment had been blotting it out all day and the metallic looking rucksack began to lift from the table where Noel had left it. Quick as a flash, Phil dashed across to grab it and deftly pressed a button on its side. The rucksack returned gently onto the table.

"It's an Anti-Gravity Pack," said Phil with a grin. He strapped the rucksack onto his back. He pressed a button and rose from the floor. He pressed the other buttons in sequence, down, up, left and right. "It's like a TV remote. The centre button's on and off." A delighted Phil flew around the room and Sarah in the shared excitement did something extraordinary for her. She clapped her hands in glee, something which had hitherto been far too painful to do.

When Phil landed, Noel said, "Let me have a go."

Obligingly, Phil took off the rucksack and handed it over. Neither noticed the sun had gone behind the clouds again. When Noel tried the buttons, nothing happened.

"Perhaps you're too heavy," suggested Sarah, grinning.

Noel scowled at her.

Marion had been watching carefully and it was only she who had appreciated that the rucksack required sunshine to work its magic. She pointed out that it seemed to need solar power to charge it. "We should leave it in the sun for some time. Tomorrow's another day and I have to meet Harry. So knock off early and go home." With that she ushered them from her office and followed them, locking the door behind her.

"See you tomorrow when we'll all have plenty to do, recording your research," she called after them as they went chattering to each other down the corridor.

At the restaurant, Harry and Marion said little until they were looking at the sweet trolley. They had drunk almost a bottle of wine between them and were, as always, relaxed in each other's company.

"It seems to me," said Marion nodding to the waitress as she pointed to the Black Forest Gateaux, "it seems obvious to me that the hologram only chose the three of us, you, me and Sarah, and we're all completely cured. That's no coincidence."

"This is correct," agreed Harry while digging his spoon into a chocolate mixture covered with double cream.

"The problem is what's the best thing to do?" stated Marion. "Should we tell the world, or a few selected friends?"

Harry pointed his empty spoon in Marion's direction. "Perhaps it'd be better to test out our theory by introducing other friends to Dr Black to see if their ailments are cured too."

"I think you're probably right," Marion conceded as she divided the dregs in the wine bottle equally between their two glasses.

"We could choose two people each – people we can trust – and then try it out in a few days' time. Agreed?"

"Agreed," said Marion, and called the waitress to bring them their bill.

17

The photographs Les Smith had taken of the writing on the stone door were front-page news throughout the world.

In Mexico City, a young boy was working cleaning shoes for office workers. He was a cheerful, amiable lad and had lots of regular customers who could see he was working hard to help his family. One day Chino, the young boy, looked up from rubbing a customer's shoes to a gleaming shine, noticed the photograph on the front page of the newspaper the man was reading, and read out loud, "Beware! Ceasurethalamus is perilous and the microscopic spores will kill to bring an end to the world as we know it."

"What did you say?" enquired the man.

To oblige him, Chino read the message again.

"How can you know what it says?" asked the man, turning the paper around to re-examine the front page for himself.

"My Grandfather taught me. It's an ancient language."

"And how would your Grandfather know?" asked the man, interested.

"He was the great, great, great, great grandson," Chino counted on his fingers, "of a magnificent Olmec King, from San Lorenzo, but the Olmec tribe disappeared thousands of years ago." Chino's pride was clear.

"My! My!" mocked the man. "An Olmec King, eh."

Chino carefully put away his cleaning equipment and held out his hand for payment. He was hurt by the attitude of this man, who had always been so pleasant when having his shoes shined over the past year. Without further comment the man passed over the necessary coins. Not realising how much he had upset the boy with his derision, he smiled and went on his way.

The man was called Jose Mimosa. He tucked his newspaper under his arm as he walked towards his place of work. He was the owner of a large company making and distributing computer programmes for industrial use. He was a smart, clean-shaven, dark-complexioned man in his early thirties, with black hair cut stylishly and smouldering dark eyes. He was dressed in a smart business suit over a pristine white shirt complemented by a blue-grey silk tie. He called every morning to have a shine put on his shoes by Chino to complete his appearance. He smiled to himself as he thought about the boy and his claim to be able to read the message baffling the international experts.

Jose was bored. His business was doing well, but although he had many acquaintances and friends, he was lonely. As he sat at his desk contemplating things, a colleague came over to talk about the news. Jose didn't mention what had happened with the shoe-shine boy. Then Harrison said he'd seen something about it in another newspaper, but couldn't for the life of him remember exactly what it was.

Later that morning Harrison gave Jose a typewritten sheet.

"What's this?"

"I rang Cara and she dictated everything in the article."

Jose read the message which Harrison had written. It included a telephone number. He took out his cell phone and dialled it. A female voice answered. Jose said, "I might be able to help decode the writing on the door of this tomb."

The woman was rather curt and explained that they were receiving many calls from nutcases who were only after the reward. "So, goodbye," she said dryly, "and thank you for calling."

"Just a minute," said Jose. "I'm not interested in a reward and didn't know there was one."

The woman at the other end of the line was still dubious. "Why do you want to disclose the information, if you don't want a reward?" she demanded.

Hastily Jose asked her if they could meet and he would explain all. "Aren't you based in Mexico City?"

Siobhan hesitated on the other end of the phone.

"Come on," cajoled Jose. "What have you got to lose? Tell you what, meet me for coffee at Marcel's Bar tomorrow at noon and I'll give you all the information that I have."

No reply.

"Deal?" said Jose, gently.

"Deal," a reluctant Siobhan replied, not because she expected him to come forward with a translation, but only because she found his voice fascinating.

Jose switched off his phone and told his secretary he would be out for the rest of the afternoon.

"Very well Mr Mimosa."

Jose felt unexpectedly cheerful as he made his way toward the shoe-shine stand. His cheerfulness disappeared quickly when the boy could not be found. He asked several nearby traders but nobody seemed to know where Chino had gone.

As Jose's enquiries continued, an old man who had been watching and listening finally approached him. He looked as though he had been living rough but had the air about him of a man who'd fallen on hard times. Jose invited him to come over the road to a café for something to eat and drink and the old man accepted gratefully. Jose ordered a coffee for himself and a meal for the old man which was consumed voraciously but with quiet dignity. The old man must have been very hungry. When he had finished, he wiped his mouth carefully with a paper serviette and sat back comfortably in his chair.

"Do you know where the slums are just off the docks?" the old man asked Jose.

"I think so," replied Jose. He watched the old man purposefully sip his coffee.

"I don't know exactly which house, but Chino lives with his mother somewhere in that area." Never taking his eyes from Jose, the old man said gravely, "I thank you."

"It is I who should be thanking you," replied Jose. "Have you been living on the street for long?" Jose enquired.

"About five years. I lost my job when I was fifty five years old and my wife took in her lover and kicked me out since everything was in her name." The summary of his personal tragedy was delivered philosophically and without any hint of malice.

Calmly Jose said, "So you're not ready to retire yet eh? What was your occupation?"

"I was a bookkeeper for James Noble and Sons, before they went into liquidation when the demand for printers became less."

"I see," said Jose. He wrote something on his business card and handed it over. The old man turned it around in his fingers to read what was written on it.

"Mimosa Building," smiled Jose, "tomorrow morning eight am sharp, and here is enough money to get you suitably fitted out for working in an office."

The old man's eyes were bright with unshed tears as took the folded banknotes and shook Jose's hand.

18

The driver was not keen on driving far into the slums. He said to Jose it wasn't safe. When he said, "This is as far as I go," Jose paid him and got out of the taxi. As he looked around him Jose could see it was a really poor area. Gangs of youths stood around on the corners of dirty tenement blocks with steps leading up to doorways in which neglected young children were sitting, staring out, hungry-eyed. A woman screamed from inside the building, but no one took any notice. Jose knew he was out of his depth and abandoned all thought of going on with it that day. He needed help. He had never really known people lived like this, day after day without hope. *I must find a way to do something about this*, he thought.

Carefully avoiding making eye contact with anyone, he walked in what he hoped would be the right direction to find another taxi. Eventually he came across a taxi stand and got a ride back to the Mimosa Building. He had reached a dead end in his search for Chino. He walked dejectedly back to his office.

Harrison popped his head around the door and asked, "Any luck with that phone number?"

"Yes and no," Jose said.

Harrison turned a chair around and straddled it, resting his folded arms on the back of it. "Tell all." The two men had been friends for years. Jose had been best man at Harrison's wedding, and two years later godfather to his daughter Scarlett, whom he adored. Harrison's wife Cara had tried a little matchmaking without any success and Jose remained firmly a bachelor.

Jose couldn't help smiling at his friend, and told him all about Chino being able to read the message and the next day's planned meeting. "Only one thing wrong," Jose said. "Chino's done a bunk, and I've only a rough idea what he told me." Jose sighed.

"I'm more interested in you meeting a young woman," teased Harrison. "Don't you even know her name?"

"No," said Jose, "I just knew I wanted to meet her as soon as I heard her voice."

Changing the subject Harrison asked, "Have you had any lunch?"

"Not yet," Jose said.

"Come on then," Harrison got up from his chair and returned it to the desk. "I'll treat you."

The next morning Harrison had interesting news for Jose. "My man thinks he's found Chino," he told Jose.

"Where? Is he alright?"

"If it is your Chino, Charlie's arranged for you to meet him at the docks at ten today."

Jose jumped up from his chair looking at his watch. He took Harrison's face in his hands, squashing his cheeks and looking him straight in the eyes, and said, "You little gem."

Harrison was caught up by his friend's excitement. "Come on," he said, "we need to get a taxi."

"We?"

"Of course, I'm coming too. I'm just getting my jacket."

The two men were quickly out of the building and heading toward the docks in a taxi. When they reached a point where it was pedestrians only, they got out and walked down the road. In the distance, Charlie could be seen waving merrily, a young boy by his side. Jose quickened his pace. Harrison did the same. When they reached Charlie, Jose put his arm around Chino's shoulder and bent down to his level. "Hi Chino, You're not in trouble so don't worry," he said.

Chino just shrugged his shoulders and looked at the floor. Not one to be put off by this reaction, Jose continued cheerfully, "Can you remember this?" He was holding out the front page of the newspaper.

"Yes," Chino said, his eyes flashing. "I remember how you insulted my Grandfather too."

"Chino, I am so very sorry," Jose said. He sounded remorseful and Chino, who liked Jose, wanted to believe him. "Please forgive me and if there's any way I can make it up to you, just say the word."

"What is it you want from me?" Chino said, suspiciously.

"All we need is for you to read the writing again," said Harrison.

Chino turned his face toward Harrison. He didn't know this man and was certainly not going to talk to him. Charlie and Jose were now both gripping Chino tightly, sensing he was about to run.

Charlie said "Chino and his Mum are leaving to go back to San Lorenzo when they have enough money for the fare."

Jose said "There's a reward for anyone who can read this." He held out the newspaper to Chino.

"It just says that it's dangerous and the spores will kill and end the world," Chino said as he wriggled free from Charlie.

"But," said Harrison "there's a long word just here. What does that mean Chino?"

Chino's eyes flashed from one to the other of the men as he stood with his hands on his hips defiantly. "My Grandfather told me that if I ever see Ceasurethalamus in this ancient language, I must return to the homeland to survive as my ancestors did many centuries ago."

"Survive? Do you mean this is really dangerous?"

"It is the end of the world," Chino said daring them to disbelieve him, clenching his fists by his side in anger.

"No one doubts what you're saying," said Jose. "All I want to do is get you your reward money."

Noticeably calmer, Chino agreed to write down the message for them. "There is no words for Ceasurethalamus. This the name given to the disease but my Grandfather told me that is what almost destroyed the Olmec people."

Jose smiled. "Thank you." He gave Chino a fat envelope.

Chino was amazed by the contents. He had never seen so much money before. Then Chino surprised them all, throwing his arms around Jose and saying, "Thank you, thank you."

Jose was astonished and gently patted Chino on his back.

The three men and boy all shook hands and Charlie said that he'd see the boy safely back to his mother.

When Harrison and Jose were returning in the taxi, Harrison asked, "Do you really think he can be believed when he says it's the end of the world?"

"He's just a kid and you know how Mexican fathers like to frighten their youngsters."

Harrison laughed, knowing that Jose was having a dig at him as a father. "One thing puzzles me," said Harrison. "How did you know how much the reward money is?"

Jose touched his nose conspiratorially. Both men laughed.

19

Jose realised he'd have to hurry not to be late for his meeting with the mysterious young lady but managed a quick shower, and a change of clothes, and still got to Marcel's Bar at a few minutes before midday. He ordered coffee from a smartly dressed waitress and every time the door opened to admit a young female he hoped it was his date but when a woman with blonde hair cascading around her face and down her back came into the bar he knew immediately that she was the one. She was wearing a dark suit with a white shirt and Jose's first impression was of long legs which went on forever and the click of her high heels as she turned and marched across the room in his direction. He stood to greet her and pulled out a chair for her.

"My name is Jose," he said, "and I am very, very pleased to meet you." He took her hand and kissed the back of it.

She seemed unimpressed, pulled her hand away, sat down and hailed the waitress. "Cappuccino please."

"And you, sir, would you like another?"

Jose didn't answer. He was too busy looking at his guest. The waitress asked again and with a slight nudge from his guest he came back down to Earth. "Oh. Err, yes please."

"I'm Siobhan." Her Irish lilt was very apparent to Jose. "I work at the university and am one of many experts who have been asked to decipher the message cut into the stone which of course you've seen in the papers." She was looking directly at Jose who couldn't take his eyes off her beautiful face.

Jose said, "I've got this for you," and passed her the paper on which Chino had written out his translation.

"We had some of this but without it all, it doesn't make any sense." Siobhan reached over the table to point out some of the words. As she did so, her hand brushed against Jose's, causing a funny little flutter in the pit of her stomach. To shake it off, Siobhan tossed her head back and her hair glinted in the afternoon sunshine beaming through the windows. She coughed to regain her composure. "This is the part which we can't understand". She was interrupted again, this time by the waitress bringing their coffees. They waited patiently for them to be set down on the table.

"Now, what was it that you were saying," asked Jose.

Siobhan gave another nervous cough. *Pull yourself together*, she thought. *Why am I behaving like the dumb blonde I'm so definitely not?* She was, after all, a woman with a first in mathematics and a career in government to prove otherwise. She couldn't for the life of her understand why in front of Jose she was acting so unprofessionally. Taking a moment to compose herself, she leaned over the table once more. "This word," she said struggling to concentrate with those smouldering dark eyes watching her every move. Jose leant closer to see although he knew exactly which word she was referring to but he too was finding it hard to concentrate, only too aware of his attraction to her and of her hazel eyes with the unusual circle of black around the iris she'd inherited from her Grandmother.

Jose told her what Chino had said about the word *Ceasurethalamus* which could not be translated, but referred to the end of the world.

"It's ancient Olmec writing," he said. "But you probably knew that already."

"No. I've never heard of the Olmecs but it's probable that their language draws words from other Indian languages but sets them in a different hieroglyphic system, which is why it's so difficult to decipher. There are similarities to old symbols found in the Valley of the Kings in Egypt. Siobhan took some papers out of her bag and showed them to Jose. "This letter here is exactly the same as that one which leads me to believe – from what we've deciphered and what the boy told you, – he's absolutely right, and there is a great danger inside the tomb; even death."

Jose nodded. "What are we going to do about it?" he asked.

"We?" Siobhan couldn't hold his gaze. Somehow he unnerved her without doing anything overt.

He said, casually, "Perhaps we should meet for dinner tonight at the El Carlos and decide. What do you think?" He was smiling broadly across the table at her.

"I don't think so," she retorted a little bit too quickly and began to gather up her belongings. She knew the restaurant he meant was the most expensive in the city.

Jose said, "Shall we say eight o' clock, then?"

Confused, she said, "Yes, whatever," turned and hurried away, treating Jose once more to the rapid clicking of her high heels on the tiled floor.

Jose made a fist with his hand and punched the air. "Yes!"

The waitress heard and turned, assuming Jose was calling her. "Did you want something else, sir?"

"No. No thank you. Just the bill please."

That evening Siobhan found herself trying on her fourth outfit. She had never usually had any difficulty in choosing what to wear. Eventually, she put on a close-fitting but simple blue dress with a sweetheart neckline, its stylish capped sleeves its only pretension toward decorative design. Her hair, her crowning glory, she swept up into a chignon using a beautiful jewelled clip to hold it in place. She wore tiny diamond stud earrings with a matching necklace and took unnecessary care with her makeup. She checked herself in the long mirror, nodded to her reflection, gathered up her handbag and wrap, and left her apartment to travel by taxi to the El Carlos.

Jose, on the other hand, had had no difficulty in getting ready. He had a walk-in wardrobe with an abundant supply of smart suits, casual wear and shirts. He dressed himself in a dark suit and white shirt with his favourite silk tie. Unbeknown to him the tie exactly matched the shade of the dress Siobhan had chosen to put on.

Jose was dropped at the restaurant a few minutes early and went to greet Siobhan who was alighting from a taxi just two down from his. Both of them noted with pleasure the punctuality of the other and smiled. Jose took Siobhan's arm to escort her to their reserved table. This gentle touch was enough to bring her out in goose-bumps. No man had ever done that to her before. Jose compounded it as they sat down by whispering to her that she looked amazing. Siobhan blushed and tried to cover her confusion by burying her head in the menu.

This brought another smile to Jose's face. "Would you like to order or are you preparing to eat the menu?"

Siobhan looked up, realising it was silly to allow herself to be so easily rattled. "Okay." A moment later and she was able to reel off her menu choices without any further ado.

After that Siobhan found Jose good company and surprisingly easy to talk to. She told him that she had passed on the information he'd given her and was awaiting further instructions. They relaxed into less significant topics and both became absolutely certain of their sexual attraction to the other. Indeed, as they talked their body language revealed their shared desire to anyone close enough to be watching them together.

At the end of the meal, both were reluctant for the evening to end. Jose asked Siobhan if she'd like to come back to his apartment for a nightcap and she nodded her agreement. The taxi took them to the Mimosa Building and, walking to the lift, heads turned to look at them but they were oblivious during their assent to the Penthouse Suite.

The next morning Siobhan was woken by the jangling of her mobile phone. She opened her eyes and with a realisation of where she was, jumped out of bed to find her handbag and answer the phone. When the call ended, Siobhan grabbed her things and headed for the bathroom. "I have to go," she shouted frantically.

Jose lazily watched her as she circled the bedroom looking for her shoes. "Can you get me a taxi, Jose? Please be quick. I'm supposed to meet my boss in a few minutes."

A couple of hours after Siobhan had so unceremoniously fled, she rang Jose to ask him to meet her urgently at Marcel's Bar. She was already waiting for him when he got there and was in a very agitated state. She had however had the presence of mind to order him a coffee already. She had also let down her hair and changed into casual clothes; a lilac T-Shirt edged with border of flowers, beige trousers and light coloured sandals.

Jose had managed without conscious effort to match her with his cream-coloured shirt and dark brown chinos. He was clean-shaven and seemed far more at ease than she was, especially after he'd kissed her before sitting down opposite her. He reached over the table to hold both of her hands. "What's the matter?"

Her wonderful eyes glistened with unshed tears. "I have to go," she said.

"What do you mean, go?"

"Back to England, and we'll never see each other again."

"When?" asked Jose, trying desperately to get his head around her news.

"Tonight," she said.

"Have you booked your flight?"

"No," she said. "Not yet."

"Don't worry, darling," said Jose. "I'll book it for you."

In her upset state, Siobhan couldn't think clearly and misunderstood. "Can't wait to get rid of me," she said.

Jose was taken aback, unsure if she had meant it or not. He shook his head. "I thought that I might fly there with you," and then added cautiously, "if you'd like me to?"

Siobhan said tentatively, "Would you? Would you really come all the way to England?" A tear rolled down her cheek.

"But of course," said Jose. "I would come with you to the end of the Earth. You don't think I'm ever going to let you go now that I've found you, do you?"

They leant across the table and kissed ecstatically, and by the time they broke away from each other were breathless with excitement. The waitress brought them back down with a bump by asking if they required anything else. They both laughed. Jose, who was if anything more flushed than even Siobhan, told her, "No thank you. Just the bill, please."

The pair left Marcel's Bar holding hands and went their separate ways only because each needed to pack.

20

Back in England, there was great pressure for attempts to be made to open the big door in the central corridor of the tomb. Most of the archaeologists wanted to wait until the message had been read and understood while scientists insisted it should be opened immediately as soon as possible to minimise the further effects of water incursion, pointing to the artefacts they had already lost to dust. Others argued that whatever was in there had been there for thousands of years and another week or so was not going to make any difference.

The debate reached new lows in the tabloids which were inviting the public to vote. Each newspaper was trying to sell more copies than their rivals by offering various prizes for the closest guesses to what the tomb contained. There were predictably any number of weird and wonderful suggestions such as valuable paintings by famous artists – Van Gogh and others of his stature, hidden there for safety during the war – or alien statues. One of the dafter ideas was that a whole living underground community would be revealed, adapted to live in that environment.

Marion and Harry had not yet been able to organise for their close friends to visit Dr Black. Without revealing their secret, it was hard to concoct a compelling reason for them to be allowed back into the chamber they'd already declared lacking in useful, recoverable artefacts. Others knew of the hologram of course but news of the dramatic cures was restricted to just five people and they didn't want to cause a riot among people wanting to be cured.

At last Marion decided to tell Mark James what they had discovered because the decision how to proceed was properly his as the Professor leading the overall investigation. He in turn became alarmed at what might arise if it became general knowledge and agreed with Marion that a lot more thought should be given to the matter before considering any disclosure.

Still pressure mounted for the guarded door to be opened.

Professor James' Mexican sources had informed him of the great danger revealed by the carved message in the tomb. At a packed meeting of the Governing Committee, he told them that the translated warning had come from a descendant of the Olmec tribe.

He was cried down and attacked for giving credence to folk memory over scientific methodology. It was pointed out that nobody had ever heard of the Olmecs. The consensus of opinion was that they should not take the word of a child who was probably only interested in the reward posted for information. The Professor asked them to at least wait until his assistant returned to demonstrate the similarities between the symbols and others found in Ancient Egypt and the territories once occupied by the Aztecs. No one wanted to listen to reason and the committee took a vote on whether to open the door now, leaving Mark James distressed by what he felt to be their absurd decision to go ahead.

The next morning Professor James complained to the Prime Minister of the danger of following the committee's decision but the Prime Minister told him that it was out of his hands. Whilst speaking that very phrase he was rubbing his hands together, as though washing them, in order to distance himself from the forecast consequences. He dismissed the Professor and told him that there was no more to be said on the subject.

That afternoon, the Professor took his granddaughter down into the cave where the hologram had been discovered. She loved him greatly and had always found him easier to talk to than her father.

Sarah said, "I'm bursting to tell you something."

"You can always tell me anything, you know that." She had always been such a fragile child and her illness had taken its toll over the years. But now he could see something different about her. Her eyes especially were gleaming and happy rather than pain-filled. For a moment he wondered if what Marion had told him might even be true, however unlikely it seemed. Perhaps it had been wrong of him to placate Marion rather than accepting that what she had said had happened had indeed happened.

"I've got a boyfriend. His name is Phil and we're in love Granddad, isn't it wonderful," a delighted Sarah confessed.

"Yes it is." The old man noted how steady her voice was and how easily she was walking. He hugged her and the cheerful pair set off down the stairs into the tomb. Reaching the closed door in the left-hand corridor, Sarah ran further down and pulled on the metal ring Phil had told her about. As before the door swung smoothly open. The lights Marion's team had erected were still in place and at the touch of a switch, the cavernous interior was flooded with light. The Professor was awe-struck. It had been a long time since he had been involved with below-deck, hands-on exploration and it gave him the same buzz as when he was a young archaeologist starting his career.

His granddaughter picked up the console which controlled the hologram. She gave it to him so he could operate it and the hologram duly appeared.

The ritual was the same as before. The handheld device was raised to scan each of them from top to toe but Sarah delightedly held up her fingers, no longer disfigured, and said "You've already cured me." Dr Black nodded to her and a ghost of a smile crossed his face. He gestured for the Professor to come closer and passed the device carefully up and down his body. The holographic man said nothing at all but the look in his eyes told the old man everything he needed to know and that there was nothing to be done for him.

Carefully they switched everything off and began the trek back to the surface, the Professor having to stop every now to catch his breath from the effort of climbing the stone steps.

The next day, amid wild media excitement, a select group of experts went back down the steps. They had all previously visited the site to determine how to open the central door, but could find nothing resembling a lock of any kind. The two excessively heavy guardian statues had however been moved to either side of the door until such time as a method could be devised to lift them to the surface.

Their best hope of opening the door, given the proven inability of modern drills to penetrate the stone-like material they were facing, was to search for a hidden lock in the walls close by. In past times, slaves had been forced to stay in such tombs to close the door from the inside. Their lives were sacrificed to ensure a huge beam was placed over registers which would then stop anyone being able to open the door from the outside. If such a strategy had been applied here then unless a secret handle was located to shift the internal beam there was no obvious way to open the massive door at all.

The men and women began a lengthy and painstaking search.

21

Siobhan and Jose flew in from Mexico. He went off to book them into a hotel, while she went straight to see Mark James carrying Chino's translation and his explanation of the meaning of *Ceasurethalamus*. Professor James asked his secretary to make them coffee and directed Siobhan to sit down. She began by telling him what she'd learned about the Olmec tribe and that, according to ancient folklore, they had survived this before.

"Most interesting," mused the Professor. "And Ceasurethalamus sounds virtually identical to the word Mrs Dewsbury attributed to her holographic man."

"A hologram?" queried Siobhan.

"Yes." He smiled at her disbelief, "Marion discovered a holographic who ran a hand-held machine over each of them to see if they had Ceasurethalamus. Nobody understood what he meant and they just went along with it."

Siobhan looked at him doubtfully.

Just then the phone rang. "Excuse me. I'll take this call next door. Drink up your coffee. I shouldn't be long."

While the Professor was gone, Siobhan wondered if Jose had managed to get a hotel room for them. Her thoughts were interrupted when Professor James came slowly back into his office, his face ashen. He sat down heavily, and took a sip of coffee before saying "They've opened the tomb. It was full of skeletons. They've already taken some up to the surface for detailed examination."

"Is that a problem, Professor?" asked Siobhan quietly.

"I don't really know, but I have a very bad feeling about it all." He took another sip from his cup and changing the subject said, "I understand you're going to be visiting your grandparents for their Golden Wedding celebrations?"

"Yes. You have a good memory," she smiled back at him, "but it's my Grandmother's best friends, Aunty Annie and Uncle Eric who've been married fifty years."

Suddenly he stood up and said quite firmly, "You must go then. Go right away."

She didn't understand the Professor's sense of urgency but promised him that she would go first thing in the morning. When Siobhan had gone he picked up his phone and dialled a well-used number. "Marion Dewsbury here."

"Oh hello, Marion I'm just ringing to let you know they've opened the tomb."

Marion was astounded. "I thought we were going to wait until we understood the message."

"I did my best but the Governing Committee over-ruled me. I even went to see the Prime Minister, but that was useless."

"What will happen now?"

"I don't know, but I don't like it at all," said Mark. Neither knew what more to say and after a long silence, Mark replaced the receiver.

Next, he called Sarah. She was so excited to tell her Granddad that she was heading north because Phil had asked her to come with him to visit his Grandmother. Mark wished her a safe journey. Given his presentiment of impending tragedy, he was glad she was getting out of London. He had only just replaced the receiver when Marion rang him back again.

"I just wanted to ask you if you're alright," she said quietly. "I sensed something when we were talking and I've known you such a long time... "What's wrong Mark?" she came straight to the point.

"I took Sarah down to see the hologram today and he just looked me in the eyes without saying anything and then nodded to me. I think he was telling me my heart's past saving. I didn't let on to Sarah."

"I'm so, so sorry Mark. Is there anything Harry or I can do to help?"

"So you've got Harry there," chuckled Mark. "About time too."

"You're changing the subject. And what do you mean 'about time too'?"

"I've been waiting years for the pair of you to see you were made for each other." Mark was laughing now for the first time in ages.

"We decided that if we're both cured, we should spend our remaining time together," Marion confessed.

"Good for you! Give my regards to Harry."

Two days later, Marion received a phone call from another colleague, Steven Nunn. After the preliminary niceties, he said, "Well, we opened the cave, and it was full of bones. I won't go into details, but there were some scrolls which are my main interest. They're written in a language I've never seen before."

"Any idea where they came from?"

"None whatsoever. It's giving me a headache just thinking about it."

"What are you going to do?" asked Marion.

"Keep trying I suppose. Remember the mystery of the bank account numbers they've never cracked for the film star Diana Dors. Well these are more difficult still and that never got solved, as far as I'm aware."

"Oh yes. I remember reading about her. Wasn't it that when she died, her only son could never get his hands on her fortune because no one could crack the code to access her money?"

"That's her," agreed Steven.

"Well, keep trying."

"So far, it seems to be about spores or something like that, but I wouldn't have thought they'd have known about that millions of years ago. That is if the carbon-dating of the bones is correct. What do you think Marion?"

"It's beyond me but if you keep this to yourself, here's something else for you to muse on. I was cured of cancer by a hologram, in the second cave."

"Good gracious," exclaimed Steven, "but how?"

"Don't know, and frankly, don't care. All I know is I'm clear of it."

"Well, if you can be cured, maybe there is still hope of me deciphering this new language. You never know. Anyway, thanks for the chat. I feel much better now."

"That's what friends are for. Let me know how you get on."

"Cheerio!" said Steven and returned his mobile phone to his pocket.

22

There was no internal beam holding the main door closed. As with the door Phil had managed to open, a well-hidden ring set in the wall did the trick but the air inside was immediately breathable without any stench of the sort they'd experienced before. A narrow passageway angled down it terminated at a wall of stones. It was difficult to negotiate the passageway, even sidling down it one person at a time. Breaking open an entrance through the wall took a great deal of effort and time but progressed steadily until the wall was breached. From the small initial opening the familiar smell issued and everyone evacuated the tomb until it cleared. Eventually, a hole big enough to climb through was cut out and a ladder secured on the other side, the chamber proving to be much lower on the inside.

The first six men, led by Peter Jones who had flown in from his tenured post in Cairo, quickly became aware of skeletons near the entrance and were at pains to avoid treading on them. "This is the same as some of the Egyptian pyramids," commented one of the men. "These were slaves left to sacrifice themselves building the wall."

The archaeologists carefully removed the skeletons from the entrance and only once this task had been achieved were the rest of the team allowed into the huge square chamber. Men and women had been invited from all over the world to be present at this major discovery and they were permitted to take samples from the tomb back to the laboratory to do some initial tests subject to oversight by Peter Jones, who in terms of professional courtesy if nothing more, would report to Professor James before passing his conclusions to the Chairman of the Governing Committee.

First, Doctor Jones examined the bones found nearest to the doorway and concurred with his colleague's impression on site that the bodies had been those of the men charged with closing the tomb from the inside. Next were the bodies discovered carefully arranged in tiers, on platforms all around the unusual, square-shaped tomb. At the far end of the tomb, the bodies had been mummified in the same manner as he had encountered when he was a young man on his earliest expeditions.

Dr Jones decided his first objective was to carbon-date his samples and the process gave him his first surprise. The results were nothing like a match for his expectations. Millions of years appeared to have elapsed between the mummified examples and the bones of the skeletons arranged in tiers on one side of the tomb and then between those samples and the bones recovered adjacent to the wall. Interestingly the most recent skeletons were all male. He could not understand the dating discrepancies but Flint, a close colleague, tasked with checking his data, reached identical conclusions. Flint also noted that, although there were many children and babies among the skeletons, there were no pregnant women. This too struck both men as odd.

Shortly after completing the carbon-dating, Dr Jones was contacted by a friend, Pedro Banderos, who was working in Colombia where he had found stone statues guarding pyramids or temple chambers similar to the English ones which he was attributing to a tribe called the Olmecs. "I could forward photographs to see if you have any views on this matter. Two heads are better than one, and the more ideas the better." He went on to say that they had found a square burial chamber with platforms to house the dead in row after row of tiers that was completely square, which he personally had never seen before. In short he described something nearly identical to the work being carried out by Jones.

"And another thing. When we carbon-dated the bones, we found there were millions of years separating the ages of the various skeletons."

"We've got the same issues here. A square chamber just like the one you've found; bodies housed on platforms and million-year discrepancies between the ages of the bones. Perhaps your Olmecs originated in my country and travelled to Columbia, or vice-versa?"

"Anything is possible," agreed Banderos. "We will have to delve further into this puzzle. Another thought, by the way, about the word you found on the tablet, *Ceasurethalamus*. *Cease* means to stop. Then, the thalamus – which of course relates to the mass of grey matter in the forebrain."

"Think that's way too literal but we should definitely compare notes. Keep in touch, won't you?"

23

Mary came to sit beside Annie for a while. Annie was beginning to get used to this young woman and, feeling rather stronger, was in the mood to talk. "Did I tell you about my husband Eric and I being married for fifty years?"

"No," said Mary. "What is being married?"

Annie explained that it meant that she and Eric had been together all that time. "It's called a Golden Wedding," she said. "Would you like me to tell you about it?"

"Yes," said Mary simply and she listened intently as Annie began her story, interrupting only when Annie mentioned things she didn't understand.

"Our closest friends Angela, Ralph, Paddy, and Sharon came to stay and help with the preparations. Sharon was so pleased because her granddaughter Siobhan managed to come over from Mexico with her boyfriend, Jose. It was the more the merrier, and Angela was going to see her grandson Philip too and by then he had a girlfriend called Sarah and they were coming. I was really pleased for them and said it would be like old times. They had always been so close when they were children and it was great they'd be able to catch up. With our Rebecca and Simon too."

"You see our grandchildren virtually grew up together. When Sharon and Paddy's son went to live in Ireland, their daughter, Siobhan, spent her holidays with her grandparents and Philip was at school in England while his parents were in Singapore so he was always around in the old days.

"Two days later and we began our celebrations. It was such fun. Eric fixed lights all around our garden and he and Paddy put up a couple of gazebos."

This was difficult to explain to Mary, but with much laughter, Annie succeeded.

"We had tables and chairs dotted around so that guests could stay in the sunshine or go into the shade. We made every kind of food you could name so that everyone could find something to their taste. Ralph was in charge of the drinks. He set up a bar so people could help themselves and he had the soft drinks easily accessible for the children. Paddy fixed up speakers so that we could have as much music as we wanted. Everyone in the street had been invited along with all our family and friends.

"Some of the young ones had decorated the whole street with balloons and bunting. I don't think anyone didn't enjoy themselves that day. Even the weather stayed warm and dry and the sun stayed out late and we got a balmy evening. We turned the music down lower as it got late and then there was a lot of smooching."

Again, this was a term requiring an explanation for Mary but when she got it, they were laughing again.

"What a time Eric and I had. John and Amanda rang us from Australia to wish us well and to say they were excited about us going over there later in the year. We put the phone onto *speaker* so everyone could hear each other. We did the same when Joanne rang. The day was a complete success as we'd heard from all of our children and grandchildren.

"But it wasn't just about the party. Our grandchildren planned on staying at least a week, and to Sharon and Paddy's delight, Siobhan was staying on a little while with her boyfriend Jose. He had such an easy manner about him and was obviously besotted with their granddaughter. Philip and his girlfriend Sarah were able to stay on a bit too. She was a very gentle girl and like a breath of fresh air for Angela and Ralph.

"After the party, the six young ones went off exploring the area together and it was great fun for them going to places Sarah and Jose had never seen; nearby castles and caves and stately homes to visit making it a great extended holiday.

"Only it was just the calm before the storm really…"

24

Mary had been enjoying listening to Annie's story until the point when Annie suddenly became very confused and upset. She was mumbling about all the people who started dying in England. Mary had no idea what thoughts were going through her mind to raise such terror in her eyes, as Annie searched around her for something familiar to cling on to. She was shaking and crying out as though in pain and so Mary helped her lie down after giving her another dose of the poppy seed potion to make sure she slept.

Annie did sleep, but fitfully, her unconscious mind focussing on everything falling apart. She couldn't seem to get back to the happier times and memories of the horrific events she'd lived through wouldn't go away.

Unexplained deaths began happening in almost every country in the world. Suddenly people were dying for no apparent reason and autopsies didn't reveal what had happened to them. The media was full of speculation because producers and editors en-masse concluded that the footage they held was too horrific to be shown to them on television. There was a particular concentration of unexplained deaths in the London area, and speculation linking the phenomenon to the removal of thousands of people to make the Thames valley safe from flooding seemed an inadequate explanation which nobody believed. Word got out about one peculiar aspect of whatever was killing otherwise healthy people; skin discolouration prior to death. *Black Death* was repeatedly cited as a possibility.

Then a demographic indicator was picked up by a statistician at the University College of London. The deaths were occurring in the young. That inexplicable fact somehow rendered the situation even more horrific.

The world began to experience a rising tide of aggression and, in addition to the mystery disease, people were dying from indiscriminate violence. Stabbings were daily occurrences, even in smaller communities, and shooting sprees were commonplace in cities. Just going out onto the streets was becoming a potentially fatal decision and law and order was breaking down in every country to a greater or lesser degree.

The British Government was not alone in issuing movement prohibition orders stopping all travel around the country until such time as the disease pathogen and mode of transition, airborne or by contact, could be determined. The army was given shoot-on-sight orders for anyone seen carrying a firearm. Being confronted by armed soldiers at every key location or crossroads was so alien that it ramped up fear still further and media hype made things worse still. Everyone feared for their personal safety.

The Government's proclamations meant that Siobhan and Philip and their partners were not allowed to return to London and had to stay put. Making phone calls was problematic too but eventually they were able to get a message to Professor James who promised to contact Jose's company in Colombia if he was able to.

The fact that post-mortems on the bodies of those who had died were proving useless as a means of determining cause of death left ample room for theories and speculation, especially as the onset of the epidemic seemed to coincide with the opening of the tomb in the old Thames riverbed and there was a clear concentration of deaths in that vicinity. The media circus now had a new approach with which to beat the Government and whip up public fury: condemnation for moving people from their homes to make way for a river, which until then had been flowing naturally, and the epidemic wholly over-shadowed earlier deaths and loss of property from regional flooding.

Professor James expressed a dissenting view, pointing out that deaths were occurring not just in England but all over the world and that it was the inadvisable removal of skeletal remains for examination by experts in various countries which provided both a nexus for the unknown disease and an explanation for its rapid international spread. Eventually, his proposal to transfer as many of the newly deceased as possible to the Thames Valley tomb and reseal it was given serious consideration. There were counter-arguments from religious and political factional interests as to the proper and spiritually respectful ways of dealing with the bodies of victims but the James Plan to contain the consequences of the epidemic was adopted, the Prime Minister going so far as to praise its clear-sighted pragmatism in a national broadcast. Prayers were offered up whilst as many victims as possible were placed in the tomb by pallbearers in full hazmat suits and then sealed inside. A day of national mourning was declared and flags were flown at half-mast on all civic buildings.

The country then held its collective breath and waited to see if the deaths stopped. Prayers and masses were said every day that went by without another reported death from unknown causes. The weather turned very cold and icy winds blew across Europe from Siberia. With relief, people began to be convinced that the worst was over and that the cold was killing whatever strange bug lay behind all those deaths.

The most draconian of the prohibition measures expired and were not renewed. Things were starting to get back to normal.

25

It seemed that Annie and Eric might be able to go to Australia to continue their round of Golden Wedding Anniversary celebrations after all, but a harrowing event caused them to think again and to bring their plans forward. They received a phone call breaking the awful news that their precious grandson Stuart was dead. John was absolutely distraught, making it almost impossible for him to talk. The cause of death had not been positively established by post-mortem leaving them baffled at how such a person in apparent good health could just drop dead so suddenly. John's parents said they would book flights out straight away.

Despite the drugs Annie had been given to make her sleep soundly, she began crying and shaking violently in her sleep. In her dreams she was beside herself with shock at the loss of their precious grandson and John seemed so fragile that, like a little boy, he desperately needed the comfort of his Mum and Dad.

The next morning, they went to the Travel Agents and received another shock. Australia had closed its borders to all foreign travellers. They tried in vain to plead that their grandson had just died and they must get there to support their family but there were no exceptions and all the airlines with routes into Sydney or Perth or any other Australian city had been grounded. Nobody was being allowed in or out of the country. Annie cried inconsolably and although Eric tried repeatedly to ring John, there was no answer.

Twenty-four hours later an Australian policeman called Dillon phoned them. As he listened tears began to run down Eric's face and his knuckles turned white from gripping the telephone so tightly.

"What on Earth is it?" said Annie.

Eric was still on the phone. "It's John and Amanda. This man says they've both died too. They can't let us fly there and the funerals will take place without us." Through gritted teeth, Eric said into the receiver, "What about our Melanie and her husband and baby son?"

Dillon said he had no news about them but would make enquiries and ring again. Eric carefully wrote down the policeman's number before returning the phone to its cradle.

Annie was on the brink of hysteria so Eric held her so tightly she couldn't move. As she regained some composure, he repeated everything he'd been told and the flooding tears came again.

When Eric had enough control of his feelings, he rang Thomas who said he'd drop everything and be with us as soon as he could using his Government pass to get round the residual constraints on travel. He also took on the burden of ringing Joanne and Jane.

Joanne couldn't come over from Canada because of similar flight restrictions to those the Australian Government had put in place. Thomas and Jenny came later the same day though and they were joined by Jane, Nigel, Rebecca and Simon. They held a wake of sorts at their local church giving them some kind of closure on the three inexplicable deaths. Thomas made email contact with Dillon, the policeman, but there was no news to be had of Melanie. There was no answer from her telephone and no one at home when he visited the house trying to locate her.

That night, Eric and Annie clung to each other, sobbing, until they fell into exhausted asleep.

In another time, Annie was also sobbing in her sleep but couldn't fully remember why.

26

On television the Prime Minister announced, with palpable relief, that there had been no reported deaths in any part of the world which could be attributed to the epidemic and the state of emergency was duly declared over. Thomas at his university laboratory was conducting tests on bone samples from the tomb to see if they could isolate the cause of the epidemic, and if so work towards creating an antidote. Things settled down into something like normal routine for most people although nearly everyone had lost someone they loved. The restrictions on flying or unnecessary movement about the country remained in place; everyone was twitchy about the epidemic returning and no one in Government wanted to be the first to say that everything was alright again. Shops were permitted to re-supply from their distribution hubs although the general population were still not allowed to travel beyond local shops and their places of work.

Joanne rang Annie and Eric to ask if they would still come over to Canada at the first opportunity once flights were restored and they agreed that was exactly what they wanted to do. *After all they were war babies and made of sterner stuff.*

Eric went into his garden and pricked out his seeds ready for planting later. "I'll have to get the planting done before we go to Canada," Eric said one Saturday morning.

"Do you want me to help you?"

"What a good idea," he laughed. "Now why didn't I think of that?" It was the first time Eric had smiled for ages. They worked well together in his greenhouse and soon had transferred a large number of seedlings into larger pots to grow on until it was time to put them out in the garden. "We make a good team," Eric said playfully smacking Annie's backside just as he used to do before they had a family. Annie flicked water at him out of the bowl in which she was washing her hands. *Laughter was a great healer.*

Normality was a short lived interlude.

The deaths started again but now the numbers were fearsome. It was mainly young children at first. The epidemic was back with a vengeance and because there were so many people dying, the only option was to prepare deep mass graves using mechanical diggers.

Throughout the world, factions were again killing people at random and a rash of car bombs were exploding. Chaos reigned. No matter how much politicians and dictators pleaded for calm, it made no difference. Rioting and looting were regular occurrences now. Properties were set on fire and from almost anywhere in the country great curls of black smoke could be seen somewhere on the horizon, if not closer to home. Then they turned the water off.

Spring came, bringing with it extremely hot weather and the smell of rotting corpses. Every day large trucks were being driven up and down streets in towns, villages, and cities to collect dead bodies. This was worse than the original plagues of the Middle Ages. This modern *Black Death* now reached pandemic proportions.

It was becoming more apparent, however, that somehow the older generation was less affected as much by the infection or virus or whatever it was. Children seemed to go first and then their parents and any ability for a community to function at all seemed to be dependent on able-bodied pensioners. It was a losing battle.

For safety reasons the gas was turned off altogether. This caused an uproar because now there was no means for most people to cook. The army was trying, but largely failing, to stop the looting and all forms of food shortages were rife. Fighting had broken out in many parts of our country over scarce resources or simply as a reaction to tension and fear.

Eventually, there were insufficient workers to maintain the power stations and electricity in its turn ceased to be available. The mobile phone network was restricted to national priority users but in any event there was no means of recharging handsets without electricity.

There had been no word from Joanne or her family since the beginning of the spring. Annie feared the worst even though Eric repeated the mantra over and over again *no news is good news.*

Neither Siobhan and Jose or Philip and Sarah had returned to London, a decision backed by Professor James in one of the last phone calls they were able to receive before silence descended on a society deprived of news other than from battery-operated or hand-cranked radios.

27

The worst was that just before the silence, Thomas was able to phone them and his news was catastrophic. Effectively it was that Annie and Eric's family had been virtually wiped out. Jenny had gone, and Jane and Nigel too. Nor could he contact Rebecca or Simon.

Thomas was very blunt. "Go to Mum's friend Alice, Dad," he implored. "Promise me that you'll go. You said you would if things got worse. Promise me, Dad."

Eric said, "I promise Son, I promise." Then the line went dead.

"I can't go on anymore," Annie yelled at Eric as though it was all his fault. He held her and made her listen to reason. "It was Thomas' wish that we go to stay with Alice and Fred, and you know I never break a promise. Do you understand?"

Annie's childhood friend Alice lived on a remote farm in a Derbyshire valley. Annie wasn't even sure if they could find their way there after all this time. For years, they had only kept in touch with birthday and Christmas cards.

They called their friends and neighbours to a meeting at their house that evening. Sharon and Paddy arrived first with Siobhan and Jose. They all hugged each other. They had been friends for so long they felt each other's grief keenly without needing words. Then Frank and Jeannie came from two doors down and Annie's older sister Barbara, the retired midwife. Next, Sam with his elderly mother, struggling to walk, crippled as she was by arthritis. The last close friends to get there were Angela, Ralph, Philip and Sarah.

"We didn't know you were having a party," shouted Angela as they came into the kitchen. Her voice was too loud and unsuccessful at masking her sadness.

"What a surprise!" Annie said.

Angela's eyes filled with tears. "We've lost them all. Except Philip...and Sarah."

"We all have," Eric said. His eyes also filled with unshed tears.

Then they had to fetch more chairs in from the kitchen as yet more people arrived. Sally, Steve, his mother Maureen, and their two young children Christopher and Paige followed by Karen and Cara who rented an upstairs flat round the corner. Then Jean and Les with their lodger Alex.

Once everyone was settled, Barbara called everyone to order. She had no family of her own and seemed able to control her emotions better than the rest of them. "We're here to decide what to do." She said.

"We weren't beaten by two World Wars and we're not going to be beaten by this pandemic, or whatever they call it today. Annie has a friend who lives miles away on a farm where Thomas thought we'd all be safe. We need to work out how we're going to get there and what we should take with us."

She was interrupted by the doorbell. Eric went to answer it and returned with a couple of strangers who were in their late twenties or early thirties. The man was in an army officers' uniform. He said his name was Jim "And my wife is Rosie. No jokes about living on a narrow boat, please. We heard you might have a plan."

Barbara explained what they were considering doing.

"I'm afraid that I've got some bad news then," said Jim.

Everyone groaned. "What now!" Sam asked loudly.

Calmly, Jim continued, "I'm home on leave and we've just had orders to stop people moving about by putting up road blocks. It's supposed to be for your own safety so germs aren't spread about from one area to another."

"Nonsense!" said Paddy. "The pandemic is spreading by itself. It's not about human contact with each other."

Jim held up his hands to placate them. "I don't agree with the orders but thought you ought to know. Anyway I could help you get past the patrols. With an army officer travelling along, we could bluff our way through. If, of course, you'd be willing to let us come with you." He put his arm around his wife as they waited for a reply.

There were nods of agreement and Eric said, "I've got a fairly large trailer we could fill up with things which we may need. Also, my car is full of fuel as I took the precaution of filling up when things looked like they were getting worse and I've not used it since. There should be enough to get us to the farm at least."

Sam said "I've got a couple of plastic containers full of petrol."

Ralph said, "I think your trailer is a good idea, Eric. We need to carry as much food as we can." He added with a wry grin, "Don't forget tin and bottle openers."

This brought a chuckle.

Barbara agreed. "That's the spirit. We can beat this thing with that attitude."

Everyone started to suggest what should be packed but Les asked if he could interrupt.

"Of course," said Barbara. "Any suggestions are welcome."

"Well," said Les nervously, "it's not really a suggestion, but me and Jean won't be coming. I don't want to dwell on the fact, but we're too old, and I'm too ill to travel and Jean won't go without me. So, we're staying put, but would you mind if Alex joins you?"

There were no objections to him joining, although Eric tried unsuccessfully to cajole Les and Jean to change their minds. They wouldn't and Cara and Karen said they'd be staying too as they wanted to try and contact their parents.

Then Barbara took back control of the meeting. She seemed to want to be in charge. She asked everyone to tell her what they proposed to bring and started a list to ensure everything was covered. Speed was obviously of the essence and departure was set for two days' time.

The next day, Sam said they should weld some kind of a cage up the sides, front and back of the trailer so they could pack more stuff in.

Eric already owned battery-powered welding gear and as they worked they had the bright idea of welding an extension out of the back so that some could ride and take a break from walking. They worked until lunch time when Sam nipped home to see that his Mum was alright. He didn't come back immediately and when Eric saw him walking slowly back up the road, he knew something was wrong.

"She's gone," said Sam, tearfully. "I think her heart gave up while I was out. Only this morning she said she wouldn't be coming with us. She must have known. I told her if she wasn't going, then neither was I and do you know what she said, Eric? She said, 'You will go lad'." He dried his eyes with a dirty handkerchief. "She must have known."

"It's probably for the best," said Eric soberly. "Tell you what. I'll call Paddy and we'll come up and help lay her to rest properly."

Sam nodded. "She always said she wanted to be buried in our garden. We can do that for her."

The three of them went to Sam's house and buried his mother wrapped in a sheet, with as much dignity as they could. Paddy said a few words over the grave before the three of them went back to the job in hand.

Meanwhile, some of the women had walked as far as the local supermarket to see what supplies they'd be allowed to buy. They were surprised to find no one there to stop them getting what they wanted although the shelves were denuded of many essentials. They brought home most of what was on their list in the trolleys, including four boxes of bottled water which they unloaded near the back door.

Sam said, "We could take those shopping trolleys to pieces and use them to build the cage. Look!"

Eric smiled and agreed it would not be such a difficult task now they had so much wire.

When the second day arrived everyone was eager to get going. "We should wait until dusk," said Paddy. "If anyone sees us making a massive exodus we'd soon have the authorities on to us."

They agreed his reasoning was sound but waiting to go was agony. No one spoke much as they were all wrapped in their own thoughts and the time dragged past. At last, they felt they could safely leave. Barbara had the last word, making everyone use the toilet before departure. As they set off she was still giving instructions that they should be as quiet as possible until they got out of the town and that they should walk in small groups so as not to draw too much attention. Annie grinned to herself. *She's still a bossy-boots.*

Eric started the engine. The tension was excruciating. He towed the trailer to the end of the street and was about to turn onto the main road when a bundle of rags appeared directly in front of him. A scrawny arm waved, motioning him to stop. "Go round," urged a panicky voice from someone in the back but suddenly Annie knew, even without seeing a face, who it was. She levered herself out of the passenger seat and ran round to the collapsed figure in front of the car, picking her up and supporting her with strength she didn't know she possessed. "Rebecca, Rebecca, you're safe now."

The others gathered to lift the girl gently into the car, Barbara vacating her seat so that Rebecca could ride.

"Don't try to talk yet," said Annie. "There'll be plenty of time later."

They travelled for what seemed like hours in short bursts and then waited for those walking to catch up. Everybody took it in turns to walk or ride. Progress was very slow. As day broke, they could see a roadblock in the distance.

Jim told everyone to walk steadily behind the car and not to be afraid. "If they turn us back, we'll find another route. They haven't got the manpower to detain us." He took the wheel and drove steadily toward the temporary barrier. The men saluted as Jim pulled up and asked him for his papers. Jim bluffed. "It's chaos back there and impossible to get a chitty in an emergency like this. I'm moving these people to the school hall in the next village for the night because their houses have been burnt down."

The sergeant saluted and said, "On your way. I think you've got enough troubles to be going on with without us making more for you." He motioned for his men to shift the barrier and was obeyed instantly.

The band of travellers went through but had gone only a hundred yards when a soldier ran after them. "Sarge says he can't see the point of carrying on stopping people moving about. We're moving out and he said I could help you if you wanted another pair of hands. I'm Liam by the way." Belatedly he added "Sir," to Jim.

"No sirs here anymore," said Jim. "You're welcome to join us."

Liam fell in at the back of the group to support the slowest walkers by carrying some of the possessions.

They had not covered more than another mile or two when they realised they were running out of fresh drinking water. Somehow, the cases of bottled water from the supermarket had been overlooked in loading the trailer. There were grumbles from those who thought that others should have noticed. Tiredness was beginning to take its toll so Jim took charge.

"There's me and Liam in uniform so the group can wait here. We'll unhitch the trailer and go and find the next place with a decent shop."

There seemed little option but to adopt Jim's suggestion although if anything happened to them the group would lose its transportation. They made camp in a little copse nearby and waited. At least they had plenty of food and whilst bringing tin openers had been a joke at first, they were only too pleased to find several of their number producing them now. It was something to grin about in adversity.

28

Liam and Jim had no difficulty in finding a supermarket but, as they drove past to reconnoitre, they spotted a couple of men outside the front doors holding baseball bats. The soldiers drove past without stopping and parked the car on a side street, getting out and circling round to the back of the building on foot, looking for another way in. They were using bushes as cover when they heard a woman scream.

As they watched a huge man came into view. He was muscled like a body-builder and was dragging a young woman across the service yard by her mop of black hair. He passed the soldiers without seeing them, intent as he was on reaching the scrubland behind the buildings. His intentions were obvious. He threw her on the ground, viciously slapping her face. "Shut the hell up."

He was kneeling astride her tearing off her top when Jim and Liam jumped in. Unfortunately for them they didn't do any real damage, merely infuriating the giant. Rolling to his feet, he swung a meaty fist at Jim catching him on the side of the head and knocking him down. Then it was Liam's turn. He managed to parry a couple of blows before being thumped with such force in the chest that he fell helplessly to the ground, all the breath knocked out of him.

He had however given Jim time to recover his feet and charge again. The result was the same as before. Jim found himself thrown down like a rag doll. He managed to drag himself to his feet in time to see his attacker bending over Liam's back, a poised knife in his hand. Jim threw himself forward, kicking the man in the head with all his strength.

It wasn't the kick itself that ended the unequal fight. It was that the man was thrown forward onto his own knife. Jim rolled the body off Liam and made sure he was breathing. Then he moved to the slumped figure of the huge assailant. Blood was pooling under the body and the man was barely conscious. Jim felt for the pulse and it weakened second by fluttering second as he died.

Jim helped Liam into a sitting position, gasping for breath, and slumped down beside him. He had completely forgotten about the girl until a voice rasped, "Thank you."

She was on her back still but her head was raised to look at her rescuers. After a moment she sat up and said, "My friend's being held in there." She pointed to the supermarket.

Jim stood. The young woman was slightly built and he picked her up easily to put her on her feet. "What's your name? I'm Jim."

"Sophie," she said.

"Right, Sophie. Where do you think your friend is?"

"The last time I saw Lorraine she was in a little office just to the right of the door down there." Sophie pointed it out to them.

"What do you reckon, Liam?"

"Use the uniforms. It's the main advantage we've got. We just walk in. We say we've got orders to inspect the place and report back to our C/O. They wouldn't dare do anything if they think we're a patrol and we'll be missed."

"That works for me. I've got my sidearm but you need to get your rifle from the car. Take Sophie back with you and leave her in the car. I'll keep watch till you get back. Can we drag this body deeper into the undergrowth before you do, though?"

When they approached, it was down the main street, directly to the front door. They reasoned that it would look more like they were on official business. A thick-set man came out to meet them.

"What do you want?" he snarled.

Cheerfully Jim walked right up to him and waved a piece of paper in the man's face before stuffing it back into his pocket. "Our Officer ordered us to check supermarkets and shops to make sure gangs aren't holding shoppers to ransom." Jim quickly added, "He only gave us half an hour to check things out and report so we'll just take a quick look inside."

This man looked at Liam pointedly holding his rifle across his chest, and muttered something under his breath which sounded like swearing, turned and led them into the building.

There appeared to be no other men inside the supermarket and as they approached the offices Jim said, "Is this where the paperwork is kept?"

"You can't bloody go in there."

It was a mistake to focus on Jim as the officer. Liam simply clubbed the man from behind with his rifle butt and he landed unconscious onto the floor.

The soldiers unlocked the door and called out Lorraine's name. "Come out. Sophie sent us to get you out." The young woman crawled out from hiding behind stacked boxes of cigarettes.

"We have to be quick." They dragged the unconscious thug into the room, locked the door and raced back to the front door, pausing only to scoop up a couple of cardboard boxes full of plastic bottles of water.

"Can you see anything, Liam?"

"No. The street's clear. Let's go."

They got back to the car without further incident. Lorraine piled in the back with Sophie and they turned round and drove back down the main street at speed, all caution abandoned. A brawny man outside the supermarket screamed at them to stop but Jim just put his foot down and now they were all laughing with relief.

"Where are we going?" asked Sophie.

"Back to the rest of our group...where you'll be safe and made welcome I'm sure," said Liam.

29

After forcing some food down, Rebecca was feeling rather better. She had had the traumatic experience of losing Simon and both her parents and had then travelled on foot, to reach her grandparents. She was dressed in her oldest and warmest clothes, hoping that nobody would look at her twice. She had witnessed rapes and killings on her journey and the thought that if she'd been a few minutes later she'd have missed them made her shudder, and she clung frantically to Annie.

As she recovered, she was able to give them some good news. "I think I'm having a baby. Simon would have loved that," she added sadly. Barbara overheard and gave her some reassurance. "You know, I was a midwife and I'll check you over. Make sure you're alright."

Later that evening Jim and Liam returned with two large boxes of bottled water and two young women. "We got in and out quickly. There was a gang there but it was cigarettes they had under lock and key. Don't think they realised the importance of water."

"Glad you brought Jim back safely," said Rosie to the new arrivals.

"You're the luckiest woman alive to have such a kind, strong husband," said Lorraine, hugging her. "We were so lucky they found us and helped us get away."

"Why did it take you so long to get back, Jim?"

"We took a rather circular route because I wanted to make sure we weren't followed."

"There's real danger out there," said Sophie. "We're neighbours and we had to run for our lives. God, and it was only this morning. Seems ages ago. They were going to burn our houses down with us inside if we hadn't got out." She ran her fingers through her tangled mass of black hair. Someone offered her a hairbrush and an Alice band to hold it in place. She grinned. "There was no time to brush it today. Lorraine doesn't have that problem." She reached over to stroke her friend's short red curls.

"Are you hungry?" asked Annie, ever practical.

"I could eat a horse," said Lorraine.

They all ate sitting around the small campfire Eric had built but it was he who then said, "I don't want to be the one to spoil the party, but we've still got a long way to go and we should get a bit further away from here."

They travelled until it was too dark to see much of anything and then camped in a rough fashion by a stream. Nobody had a comfortable night and the children especially, Christopher and Paige, were uncharacteristically fractious, until they fell asleep.

The problems continued as they travelled on the next day. Sally tried her best to calm them down, but they were aggressive and disrespectful to her. Steve, their father, forcefully sat them down to try to soothe them but as soon as he let them go, they were charging about, up and down the line of straggling travellers, screaming as they ran.

Both Sally and Steve had been at their wits end all day anyway since Maureen, Steve's mother, had been complaining of severe pains in her face and her arms. She was not the sort of person to complain and to hear her sobbing with pain distressed everybody.

Sally was so exasperated with the children that she made Steve have another go at them. He tried to explain that their Grandmother was ill and they could all do without misbehaviour from them. Christopher pulled a face. "You can't send us to our rooms 'cause we don't have any, anymore." Paige wasn't much better, following her brother's lead. Eventually when they next stopped, the only thing Steve could do was insist they both got into their sleeping bags and he stayed by their side until finally they both did fall fast asleep.

When everyone had settled down for the night, Sally sat up with Maureen and they were drinking some milk when one of the children called out, as though in pain. Sally went over carrying a torch. There was no sound from them now and when she illuminated them she screamed. Maureen struggled to her feet to see what the matter was, clutched at her chest and fell to the ground.

The noise woke everyone. They found Steve cradling his dead mother in his arms and Sally wailing over the children. Each had died clutching their heads, their eyes bulging from the sockets in a horrible manner.

Rebecca got hold of Annie's arm and gently but firmly led her away from the scene. "Come on Grandma. It's not necessary for you and me to be here."

Annie said, "This must be how the rest of our family went."

"Try not to think about it, Grandma. We have to survive."

In the morning Steve announced that they were going back. He told them not to try to change their minds because they had never been completely happy about leaving home in the first place. Before they left, the men dug a grave for the three bodies and then Steve and Sally walked away without as much as a backward glance.

30

The going was slow because they could only travel at the pace of the slowest person. It took them many days and seemed nightmarishly longer. During the day, they saw the scale of devastation and death that was being brought by the pandemic upon every town and village. Each of the travellers kept their own counsel from a sense of self-preservation. The stench of rotting bodies, and the fact that they were helpless to do anything about it, was frightening. They tried not to look, but the images of all those dead eyes remained in their heads. It was difficult to negotiate their way through the towns they were compelled to travel through. They could see houses burning and the acrid smell of burning flesh filled their nostrils. The quicker they got out into the countryside again the better they felt.

Someone had relieved Eric from driving and as they walked Annie was talking about a television programme they had seen a long time ago. "It was about some soldiers and the progress they were making toward their own lines, away from the enemy." Eric shrugged his shoulders and continued plodding onwards.

"Don't you remember it? It was long before the pandemic."

"Yes. I think I might do. Why does it matter?"

"There was a part showing a long line of refugees wandering slowly and aimlessly, away from the fighting."

"I remember the enemy aircraft strafing them as they tried to escape," said Ralph, who was immediately behind them on the road.

"Yes, I remember that." Eric finally joined in. "Every foot of the roadway was strewn with bodies. Men, women and children were killed and there was no escape from the aeroplanes flying over and firing at them." Eric put his arm around Annie and gave her a warm hug, acknowledging her depression. For days they had been witnessing similar scenes to this and as in that film, there had been no able-bodied people to bury the hundreds of dead, and they had been left by the wayside to decay. It was horrible and the worst of it was when they had to take a road through a town or village and Mike and Frank, or the other young men, had to tie scarves around their faces and wear gloves so they could move the decomposing bodies from the path of the car and trailer.

Somehow they were all coping as well as they could but it seemed strange now to realise the street where they'd lived had kept them insulated to a considerable degree from how bad things really were.

They settled down in yet another copse of trees and bushes where they felt reasonably safe to stop, eat and rest. Jim organised sentries to watch over the others while they slept. He said he didn't really expect any trouble, but it was as well to be prepared and Eric had covered the car with a few branches so that when the sun rose, it wouldn't glint off the glass. Most of them were fast asleep when they were woken rather roughly by Alex, one of the men on guard. Jim held his finger to his lips in a signal to be quiet and they waited in trembling silence. Nothing happened for several minutes but then three people walked into the middle of their resting place and were quickly grabbed and wrestled to the ground, crying out in surprise and shock. When a torch was produced, they turned out to be no threat at all but three women, sapped of strength and clearly exhausted.

A few seconds later a young boy came rushing into the copse wielding a big stick. "You leave my Mummy alone," he yelled swinging the branch around his head. Frank grabbed him and took the stick away from him. One of the women rolled over and called out, "I told you to stay under cover didn't I?"

Jim very quickly assessed the situation and took charge. "No one's going to hurt you. You are safe now."

The boy squirmed out of Frank's grasp and ran into his mother's arms. Frightened eyes darted about, looking from one to another of the bedraggled group of travellers to whose encampment they had blundered. Jim stepped forward to help one of the women from the ground, but she cowered, holding onto her companion for protection. It was Rosie whose soothing voice persuaded them that they were safe. She offered them something to eat and drink and when it was produced they consumed it greedily, still on the ground, human beings reduced to animal desperation.

The woman with the boy finally said, "Thank you," but when she stood up, she wouldn't let go of her son. The other two also clung together, traumatised by the cruelties they had so recently endured.

Since they were all now awake and because it was almost dawn, Jim suggested that they move on. The exhausted women and the child were persuaded to ride in Eric's car and the group carefully packed up their belongings, making sure to leave no evidence that they had ever been there.

Jeannie was walking alongside Alex that day and they stopped at an abandoned shop full of rolls of material. "Let's get as much as we can carry," said Jeannie.

"What are you going to do with it?" asked Alex.

"It'll always come in handy," Jeannie replied.

They went into the shop cautiously and when they were sure no one was about, they carried roll after roll out and had the others pile it onto the trailer. There were rolls of terry towelling of every colour: navy-blue, bright red, yellow, green and more. There also was thick woollen material too, undoubtedly serviceable for warm winter clothing.

"We need to get plenty of these too, so we can sew things," said Jeannie, handing Alex an armful of cotton reels. "I'm just going to have a look around to see if I can find needles as well." She rummaged at the back of the counter until satisfied that they had collected enough to meet any immediate future need.

By the fourth week they didn't know how much longer they could keep going. Tiredness was making them all bad-tempered. "How much further?" was the most common question asked and "Are you sure you know where we're going?"

It was, according to Liam, typical behaviour when strangers enduring hardship were thrown together for a protracted period of time. Jim said it would pass. After all, things couldn't any get worse.

31

Rebecca started being sick. Barbara checked to make sure she wasn't having problems carrying her baby. She took her away from everyone else so they could have some privacy and she came back expressing the view that Rebecca's symptoms were a normal part of her pregnancy.

The mother of Ben, the stick-wielding child, was called Marion and she asked Barbara to look at her too because she thought she might be about three months gone too. By the time Barbara had examined Marion and both her friends, it was confirmed that the group now included four mothers to be.

By now, they had all begun to work out that older people and pregnant women seemed to possess some natural immunity from the spores, or whatever was causing the killer disease. Some men seemed to survive, but none of them could offer any explanation for this. Barbara asked if there were any other expectant mothers in the group and was surprised to add both Sarah and Siobhan to that select band.

The group now had a reason to celebrate even if it did so fairly quietly so as not to attract any unwelcome attention.

They travelled another day, and that night were surprised to find that following Eric's mapped-out route was taking them off tarmac roads, and onto a cart-track in the heart of the Derbyshire countryside. It appeared they had reached their planned destination. The group stopped to rest while Jim and Liam went on to see what was up ahead. They came back with the news that there was indeed a house at the bottom of the track, nestling in the valley and sheltered by huge trees.

Following the track a few hundred yards more brought them in sight of a farm amid a great crescent of trees with bluebells clustering around them. Beyond the farmhouse was a wide plain, and in the distance, purple-heather covered hills. The scenery was beautiful and completely untouched by the disasters afflicting every other place they'd travelled through. It was a complete contrast to the horrors of the last few months.

Everyone stood in awe, looking around at what they hoped would be their own safe haven. Drained as they all were from their journey, their haggard faces were wreathed in smiles.

Eric hugged Annie tightly, telling her that this meant they'd kept their promise to Thomas.

Annie pointed to their pregnant granddaughter standing a little away from them and said, "This isn't the end at all. It's a new beginning."

Bringing them down to Earth, Jim suggested that they leave it to Eric and Annie to go the rest of the way before the rest followed. For them all to descend upon the farmers could be too much of a shock. The travellers were exhausted from the journey in any event and making camp where they were seemed the best idea from everyone's perspective.

Eric and Annie went carefully down the winding track. Cautiously, they closed the six-barred gate behind them in case there were dogs on the loose. They had no prior warning at all when a harsh voice shouted, "Who are you? What d'ye want?" They swivelled and at the corner of the barn two men, one very elderly and the other young enough to be his grandson, were standing motionless, shotguns at the ready.

Annie was so scared, her voice came out as a mere squeak.

"Speak up woman, or clear off!"

Eric took over, calling back loudly, "We're here to see Alice and Fred and the girls."

Then something quite unexpected happened. The old man lowered his gun and began to cry. The other man plainly had no idea what to do under the circumstances and he also lowered his gun as Annie and Eric closed the gap between them.

They stopped a few feet apart and Annie said, "You're Mr Harris aren't you? We used to come and visit you and Alice years ago."

"It's Annie isn't it?" said the old man extending his free hand to grasp her shoulder. "I'm sorry, lass," he groaned through gritted teeth and tears. "I should've known who you were without scaring the wits out of you."

"What's happened, George?" Eric asked putting an arm around the old man's shoulders and patting his back.

"Alice and Fred took the girls to visit Disneyland in Orlando, and then they couldn't get back 'cause the planes stopped flying." George was sobbing unashamedly into Eric's neck now, holding onto him for dear life.

"I know, I know, we've all lost our families," said Eric.

George drew himself up to something approaching a long-forgotten military stance. "Where are my manners?" he said. "Come inside. I bet Wendy's got the kettle on. Come on Martin, you too." He strode purposefully to the kitchen door, and as he opened it, two collie dogs came bounding out to greet them.

32

Jim and Liam watched the scene unfold from the hillside. "If we're all going to be staying here," said Jim, "we're going to have to do something about security."

"I agree," said Liam. "The old man knows that too. That's why he had a shotgun. But what can we do?" Liam shrugged his shoulders.

"Maybe turn this into a vantage point, and use it to give us warning of intruders and marauders. That's for starters. Must be other steps we could take if we put our thinking caps on."

"A fence across the track and some quick-growing flora to cover it," suggested Liam. They made their way back to the others, getting ready for another night under the stars, and to the smell of food heating on an open fire as it wafted in the air, and to the muffled clatter of pots and pans.

Wendy had, indeed, got the kettle on. She recognised Annie at once and hugged her and Eric in turn before she rattled the cups onto the table. "And this is Martin," she said. "He came up here months ago with a tanker fuel and stayed when he could see we needed help because he had no one to go back to."

They sat at the old kitchen table sipping their tea and telling each other what had brought them to this place and time.

"I remember Thomas," said George. "He was taller than me the last time I saw him when you and your family came for a holiday. How old was he then, about twelve?"

Before George could make any other comment, Eric turned to him and in a choking voice told him of his last conversation with his son.

"Oh, my lovelies, I'm so sorry, of course, you must stay here," said Wendy.

Annie said, "Our Thomas was working as a scientist at the University Laboratory and knew a lot about this damn pandemic." As tears ran involuntarily down her cheeks she added, "We've lost most of our family too, Wendy. But we still have Rebecca, our granddaughter."

Wendy refilled Eric's cup and Annie nudged him, urging him to tell them about the others.

"I was just coming to that. We've left a right ragtag group of travellers camped near the lane end, all hoping to find some respite from the horrors we've been suffering these last months."

George said, "We're not doing a great job running this farm by ourselves. Why don't we eat some of Wendy's fine stew and worry about sorting your friends out tomorrow and you can have a good wash in hot water and a decent sleep in a proper bed."

Annie and Eric were delighted at the prospect. It sounded like heaven.

Things did look better the next morning. The sun was up and bright in the sky as Eric, Martin and George went up the hill to meet the others. George was taken aback by the number of people at first, but walked among them, shaking hands with the men, and kissing the women on the cheek.

Back in the farmyard the travellers walked into the luscious smell of eggs and bacon wafting from the kitchen. Among the attributes the farm had was a surfeit of hens, a diesel-powered generator and a huge chest freezer full of meat. Soon a huge party was in progress with everyone laughing and talking and eating all at the same time.

While Barbara and the rest of the elders took up quarters in the spare farm bedrooms, Jim and Liam asked George if it would be alright to set up home in one of the barns. George had Martin take them to the largest which had solid stone walls and contained only a minimal amount of farm machinery while he took Mike as a willing volunteer out to the orchard to see to his bee hives.

First, the travellers set to work clearing out all the rubbish and then the women swept the floor. It was a huge task and the dust was choking, until Margaret, Mike's wife, came up with the idea of sprinkling water over the dusty floor so it wouldn't blow about as much.

Meanwhile Frank went off with Liam to find materials they could use to build partitions to give some privacy while Phil and Jose clambered over the corrugated iron roof repairing holes. There proved an obvious solution to the creation of internal walls in the shape of huge sheets of polythene which had been used to cover bales of hay. Affixed to wooden frames they made ideal space-dividers.

Everyone worked hard all morning and fully deserved the late lunch Sharon, Annie and Wendy served up in the farmyard. The weary labourers washed at the trough in the yard and then devoured the stew put before them sitting on wooden benches in an atmosphere of positive chatter and more laughter. It was something none of them had experienced in a long time, and people returned to their chores with lighter hearts if heavier bellies. By late afternoon, the barn had been turned into a comfortable and moderately clean place to sleep.

Whilst the others were allocating the sleeping quarters, Martin led Alex over to the far side of the farmhouse to see what could be done about extending the toilet facilities. Martin said, "We had to stop using the toilets in the farmhouse because the cess pit overflowed. We couldn't empty it so I made this outside latrine from what I could remember of films I saw when I was a lad. It's plenty good enough for the three of us, but we'll need to build more now with so many extra people."

Martin's construction was a fair distance from the house and contained a hole in a raised wooden box, the back of which was an open drop into the valley below. "I built it here so that the effluent would gravity-feed into the valley."

"You mean it just flows out the back," said Alex. "We could build some more of them but I suggest we put them nearer to the elderberry trees. I read somewhere that they are supposed to keep the flies away."

"Okay," agreed Martin. "I'm open to all suggestions."

The next morning they collected tools from one of the outhouses and set about the task. There was a lot of sawing and hammering but by the time they were called for lunch they had made good progress. By late evening, they had built three more respectable toilets with a shed-like covering and a door to each. They stepped back to admire their work, before joining the others to announce what they'd built and to invite their friends to stop trekking over to and queueing for the old latrine. Privately Martin and Alex agreed that at some future point they'd see if they could find a way of draining the old sewage pit but for that they'd need an industrial pump and a tanker of some sort. "We can dream," said Martin.

Most of the men and some of the women crowded into the farmhouse kitchen that evening to catalogue the resources available to them and to discuss the vexed issue of security.

Food would become an issue in time but for now they had greenhouses yielding lettuce, tomatoes and cucumbers, a field of potatoes and Wendy's carefully-hoarded stockpiles: a huge quantity of rice, the contents of the meat freezer and another freezer in which Wendy had stored surplus vegetables including peas and sweetcorn.

They still had electricity from wind turbines which Fred had fitted, and solar panels on the farmhouse roof. When mains water had been turned off, Martin and George had welded together a substantial tank, which they filled with rainwater and from the river. This meant they had all the hot water they required even if drinking water needed to be boiled on the Aga hob.

Survival was beginning to look achievable if onerous but Jim and Liam in particular wanted to be sure what they had at the farm could not be stolen by outsiders. The inventory of available weapons included Liam's rifle, three shotguns, Jim's army pistol and a small bore-hunting rifle George kept for rabbiting. "Okay for now," pronounced Jim, "but we'll need to supplement that lot. And forage for more ammo."

To celebrate the arrival of *the wanderers* as George called them, he had been down into the cellar and fetched up several bottles of his daughter Alice's homemade wine. That went down well but more popular still was Wendy's announcement that if they'd like to take buckets down to the stream and fill up the water tank, it would be possible for each of them to take a hot bath or shower. A cheer went up, and there was a mad scramble for buckets, and a race down to the river. A few hours later and the whole lot of them were merrily sloshed on homemade wine and cleaner than they'd been in a very long time. The women particularly kept telling Wendy how wonderful it felt to have washed their hair.

Over the next few months, specialisms developed by way of chores. Mike was gradually taking over the apiary from George; Eric and Paddy were happily growing things in the greenhouse and garden; Heather and Cynthia had discovered a preference for animal husbandry and became adept at milking the cows and goats. Sophie and Lorraine had formed a close partnership with Jim's wife Rosie and the three of them worked a couple of the fields. They could all drive the tractor, and with some instruction from George had set about planting more potatoes, carrots and cabbage. They had a section of wheat too and if they proved successful in growing it they intended to make flour for bread. Someone had told them that it was possible to keep yeast alive to use again and again and Wendy had a small stock of dried yeast for future experimentation.

The most restless in their quest for new successes were Frank and Liam. Their current project was a scheme to get the old well working. The only drawback was that when they lowered the bucket into the well, they never got water, only mud. "There's only one thing for it," said Frank cheerfully. "You'll have to lower me down to the bottom of the well so I can find out what kind of a problem we're looking at."

Liam said, "Rather you than me, son. It's a long drop." They knew that because they'd dropped pebbles down it, counting off the seconds until they reached the bottom.

Frank carefully settled himself into the bucket. "Good job I'm only little," he chuckled.

"Shame you're so bloody heavy," was Liam's response. He tied the end of the rope off around a tree so that he had more control and let the rope out gradually to lower Frank down the well. When Frank reached the bottom, he pulled on the rope twice, the agreed signal. It was very muddy so some water must be getting in *but from where*? He shone his torch onto the walls and scraped away at one of the lowest bricks. It came away in his hand, and he yelled as a spray of dirty, cold, muddy water shot out, hitting him full in the face and soaking his clothes. Liam tightened his grip on the rope and began to haul him up.

"Stop!" shouted Frank.

Liam stood stock still. "Are you alright?"

"No problem. Just give me a bit longer, but put me back on the bottom first."

He pulled on other bricks and tucked them into his bucket. Water began gushing through the gap, so he tugged on the rope three times, the signal to bring him back up.

As Liam tugged and pulled on the rope, he was joined by Martin who was passing. Between them, they hoisted Frank to the surface and he appeared, grinning like a Cheshire Cat. His face was completely covered with mud, making a complete contrast to his pearly white teeth and at the sight of him Liam fell about, convulsing with laughter.

They secured the rope and helped Frank out of the bucket. Martin said, "What happened?"

"Oh, nothing much," said Frank. "Just thought I'd take a cold shower and a mud bath but I reckon that if we leave it a couple of hours, it should fill up. If not, then I'm sending you down."

Liam didn't have to go down. The water flowed and settled sweet and clear. The problem of drinking water was solved.

There were two other skilful experimenters. Phil and Jose were equally adept at making things work. They found a couple of millstones and with a bit of ingenuity, rigged them up so that they could get one of the animals to walk round and round, pulling the top stone over the bottom one in order to grind whatever wheat Rosie, Lorraine and Sophie managed to grow. They didn't have to wait for the crop though because Wendy pointed out that the silo behind the barn was already full of grain. "So, if your idea works, we can produce flour right now."

The first trial batch of brown loaves, a touch on the gritty side but edible, appeared two days later.

33

Jeannie had set herself up at the far end of the sleeping quarters in the large barn as this was the cleanest place to use Wendy's treadle sewing machine. She was surrounded by terry towelling material cut into the shape of small, drawstring trousers. She had consulted with the other expectant mothers and all had agreed that trews would be preferable to nappies because no one had any safety pins to hold them in place. Rebecca said they could make some bigger ones for when their babies learnt to walk with an attached bib and shoulder straps to keep them up like dungarees.

Before any of the babies were born, Alex came by to see how Jeannie was getting along with the sewing. He said, "I thought you were going crazy that day when you insisted we collected all those rolls of material. And now..." he gestured to the pile of new miniature clothes, "the babies would have been in a mess without them."

Jeannie laughed. "No pun intended."

"Oh! I see what you mean," Alex said when the penny dropped.

Life fell into a pattern again, and they were all blossoming. Barbara, in her late eighties, was enjoying explaining the rudiments of childbirth to all the young pregnant women. Where possible she drew them diagrams so that if she was unavailable each of them would have some idea what to do. "Not that I'm planning on popping off anytime soon," she said.

Six months after reaching the farm, Rebecca was the first to go into labour. Barbara praised her for her timing because she started around midday rather than in the middle of the night. Some of the other mothers wanted to stay and help but Barbara was having none of it. "Don't you lot have something better to do?" she said in a matronly voice which brooked no argument. They scattered and left Rebecca's great-aunt to it.

A few hours later and everyone was drawn to the barn by the cry of a new-born. A great cheer went up when Barbara announced that the baby was a boy. A tired mother slept unaware of all the attention her new son, Thomas, was getting. Rebecca had always said if her baby was a boy he'd be called Thomas after her brother because he was the one who had directed them to their haven. Eric and Annie were particularly excited to be holding their great-grandson. Eric put his finger close and Thomas immediately clutched it, bringing a tear to Eric's eyes.

As soon as she was up and about again, Rebecca went to find Jeannie. "I wanted to tell you the towelling pants you made are a big success. Thank you."

A few weeks went by and then several more babies were born one after the other. When Marion's labour pains were becoming stronger, she asked, "Where's the gas and air?"

"No such thing now I'm afraid," laughed Barbara. "We're truly back to nature, so just push when I tell you."

Marion kept saying, "This is much tougher than when I had Ben."

Barbara told her that when she first started midwifery they were told to stand no nonsense from the mothers and definitely no screaming as it would frighten the prospective fathers.

This made Marion laugh and she gave an almighty final push and her baby was out. It was a girl, whom she called Susan after her mother, and her young son Ben after shyly arriving at her bedside seemed quickly smitten by his new baby sister.

Then it was the turn of Heather and Cynthia. They had gradually become less fearful human beings and had gained a joint identity as *the milkmaids*, because they enjoyed looking after the cows, and both carried on right up to going into labour. Oddly they both went into labour almost simultaneously.

Barbara was quickly on hand reassuring them she was well able to cope in the old fashioned ways. "When I started we didn't have scans and we had to measure the bump to see if everything was in order. I must have known something like this was going to happen because I packed my nursing bag before anything else."

"Did you really know?" asked Heather, naively.

"No child," said Barbara. "I treasure this bag more than anything else, and I couldn't bring myself to leave it behind."

"Oh!" was all Heather managed between instructions from Barbara to push.

Heather's baby was another girl, Chloe, while her friend Cynthia gave birth only half an hour later to a boy, James. She too had been very frightened and in need of Barbara's stories to distract her.

"Did you know?" Barbara asked Cynthia, "this bag was bought for me by a very special man in my life."

"Was he your boyfriend?"

"No, he was the very first male midwife ever, and everybody made his life hell. I befriended him and to show his appreciation he gave me this leather bag, which I wouldn't have been able to afford for years and years." She sighed, "Enough of this reminiscing, or I'll be crying. Now pant like I've taught you."

Barbara left Angela to clear up as she went for a well-earned rest and Angela, while folding up the cloths which had been used, made the mistake of asking Cynthia, "Was James the name of the baby's father?"

Cynthia started to sob hysterically. Angela stepped back, shocked and with no idea what to do. Heather, the stronger of the two women, rushed to her feet to calm her friend but Heather was also in tears as they clung to each other. Angela stood beside them wide-eyed, not understanding their hysteria.

"Our babies both have the same father," Heather said in disgust, and she spat on the floor.

Like a thunderbolt, realisation of what had happened to them before they all met up so abruptly at the group's campsite struck Angela. She circled them with her arms. "You're such brave, brave girls."

Sophie, when her turn came, woke Barbara late in the night. "I think I'll be in need of your assistance," she said, shaking the old woman awake. "Sorry but I don't think I can wait 'til morning." Then, everything happened very quickly, and Sophie gave birth right there on the floor. Sophie kept saying sorry, over and over for not giving Barbara more warning.

"Stop saying sorry child," commanded Barbara. "The only thing I'm cross about is having to get down on my knees." She called for help and Angela came bustling quickly into the room. A few minutes later, the second of the twins arrived.

"I thought about calling them after my rescuers Jim and Liam, "but one of them's a girl. I think it'll have to be Lois and Liam." The twins were as beautiful as their mother with the same olive coloured skin and brown eyes. Both had a mop of black curly hair which would probably be as unruly as their mother's was.

Angela had helped Barbara with a few births now, and she made Barbara sit while she finished things off. Wendy called upstairs to ask how many wanted a cup of tea, as she'd got the kettle on. "I'll have water please," called back Sophie. "Hang on to the tea, it won't last forever."

Downstairs, Barbara flopped onto a chair in the kitchen. She may have been old, but for all the mothers to be she'd been a tower of strength. As she sipped her tea, she told the rest of them, "Six babies are enough to be going on with, for the present."

"Sorry to disappoint you Barbara, but I think I'm in labour too." A smiling Lorraine put her head around the kitchen door. "There's no rush. I'm sure that you can finish your cup of tea first."

Sharon was up already as well and nudged Wendy. "We might as well start cooking breakfasts," she said. They were getting adept at rustling up meals for large numbers of people. Sharon expertly flipped eggs in the huge frying pan and smiled at Angela, who had come downstairs to help after settling Sophie and her babies to rest a while. "Don't think so." Sharon hooked a thumb in Lorraine's direction.

Angela did a U-turn and escorted Lorraine upstairs, telling Barbara to finish her tea, at least until the actual birth was closer. Barbara smiled, nodding her approval. A few hours later, Barbara was able to tell everyone that the latest arrival, Josh, was doing really nicely too.

34

Jose and Siobhan were blissfully happy to be at the farm despite how hard the physical work was. They were inseparable, and both were thrilled at the pregnancy. Jose asked Siobhan to marry him one warm summer evening as they were walking over the fields among the cows grazing the clover. He said he wanted the child to have his name and, just because life was a little different now could see no reason why they shouldn't get married.

"Put like that, how can I refuse," said a grinning Siobhan. "Let's hurry back and tell the rest of them. They could do with something else to focus on except work." They practically ran, or in Siobhan's case wobbled, back to break the news.

First, they told Siobhan's grandparents, who were as thrilled as they were, and then the rest of the group. In the blink of an eye, preparations were being made and Wendy sorted out her daughter's wedding gown. "Can't have a wedding without a dress, can you?" she said, as she shook out the beautiful gown. Rebecca wanted to see her in it so she could make the necessary adjustments and they were in full swing, when someone asked, "Who's going to perform the ceremony?" Siobhan was devastated. This obstacle hadn't occurred to her or to Jose.

Sam came to the rescue. "As well as being a butcher and all the other jobs I've done in my life, I was a lay preacher. If that will do," he said, "I'm your man." Siobhan kissed him on the cheek, which made him blush.

The great event took place a week later and it wasn't one simple wedding. Siobhan had taken it upon herself to suggest something to Sarah and Philip. "Why don't we make it a double wedding? What do you think?"

Phil said, "We thought about suggesting that but we didn't want to push ourselves into your special day."

"Nonsense!" said Jose. "A pleasure to have you on board," and shook the other man's hand.

It meant Wendy cheerfully surrendering her own wedding dress. "It's a bit old-fashioned, but I loved it."

Sarah was overwhelmed. "It's beautiful," she said, a glistening of tears in her eyes. She tried it on and was surprised to find it a near perfect fit despite her bump.

Wendy smirked wickedly. "Good job I was well-built like you when we got married," she said. She quickly turned her attention to the contents of a large, wooden chest from which she extracted a huge family bible, "And this should help Sam with the service."

The day arrived, and Sam performed the service perfectly. The brides looked as beautiful as every bride should; there was singing and dancing until late that night; the wine, which Margaret had been brewing for a long time, was flowing, and efforts had been made to vary the food as much as possible, to make the day even more special. They were all were understandably reluctant for the day to end.

Two weeks later, Sarah had a son whom Phil called Adam after the First Man and awhile after that Siobhan and Jose became proud parents to their daughter, Mary, the cause of and excuse for more celebrations.

35

Rebecca came scurrying into the kitchen full of excitement. "What do you think of these Gran?" She was holding a couple of jars.

Sharon said, "If they're intact my girl, we've hit the jackpot."

"I thought they looked okay, and there are lots more in the other barn over there."

"You shouldn't be in there," said Annie. "That the old roof could fall in any time."

Rebecca said, "Don't fuss. I'll get some of the others to help 'cause there's lots more." She dashed off, leaving the two old women staring at each other.

As Sharon washed the jars, she sighed. "The rubber seals have perished. They're pretty useless."

Wendy stirred. She spent more and more time dozing in her chair these days. "We used beeswax, when I was a little girl. Don't know how it was done but I expect one of you will figure it out." The next minute, she was asleep again.

When Rebecca returned it was with Frank's wheelbarrow full of jars.

"Alright," said Sharon. "I'll go and check with Mike if we can use beeswax before I wash that lot."

Angela piped up excitedly. "If we can bottle some of the produce, it'll see us through the winter. We can't exactly just pop down the shops anymore."

Annie said, "Let's have a drink and think about it, the kettle's boiling." They had become quite partial to nettle tea as a substitute for the long-expired stock of the real thing.

When Jeannie went into labour, Barbara was still on hand to assist, although it was touch and go, as she'd been struggling to get over a nasty cold. Margaret had made some rose hip syrup and mixed it for her with honey and lemon juice. "I'm not quite sure of the recipe and it may taste bitter, but drink up! This will either kill or cure you, as my old Granny used to say."

Barbara felt so wretched, she didn't care what it tasted like and certainly within two days she was feeling miraculously improved. Angela said she was relieved. She didn't want to be left with sole responsibility for delivering Jeannie's little daughter.

There were no hitches and Frank was beside himself with pleasure to be holding Megan in his arms. They'd been lucky to manage so many births without losing a child and their good fortune continued with Craig's arrival to a disbelieving Margaret. "It must be all this country air," confessed Mike.

The last one to go into labour was Rosie. Her infant was simply ruddy with good health from the second she arrived, a solid eight pound bundle of energy. "Not sure it's the most appropriate name for her," said Jim, "but we chose in advance. Ethan if it was a boy and Emma for a girl. So we'll stick with that decision."

Twelve healthy babies had all been born within the last few months, and the beauty of that was they'd all grow up as playmates together.

Life on the farm began to fall yet again into a regular pattern. During the summer and autumn, they used the Kilner jars to bottle foodstuff for the coming winter. The fruit in the orchard would follow but it was too early to be picked yet. They had already learnt to spread the apples out in the roof space of one of the barns, not touching each other, and with regular checking they managed to save most of the crop. The windfalls Margaret put to good use to make cider, a welcome community asset.

The children were growing fast. Clothing and footwear for everyone was fast becoming a problem. Ralph had the idea of drying out cow hide. "If we stretch it out in the sun and scrape it, like the Indian women did in the old Cowboy films, we'd have some kind of leather."

Paddy agreed. "I saw that in the films and I think we should be able to make moccasins with a bit of thought."

The two of them went to see Sam to find out when he'd next be slaughtering a cow. Sam said it was not a problem because they were in need of more meat. "Maybe, you could use sheepskin too," he suggested. "It would be warmer with the fur left on."

By the next day the three men had skins stretched out to dry on newly constructed racks.

Ralph's feeling was that it was going to be a productive move. "We may not make leather as good as our shoes used to be, but we'll give it a good try and we can soften it with the cooking oil you've got by crushing seeds," he said.

"It seems you've hit on a good idea," agreed Eric.

"And I could do with something else to wear on my feet," said Angela. "Can you make moccasins do you think?"

"We can but try."

The winter passed remarkably easily. The effects of Global Warming, which they'd been warned about in another life, were less severe than predicted but winter was the warmest anyone could remember, and then early spring gave rise to a promise of a good summer with just enough of the precious rain they needed.

There was a lot of laughter around the farm. The young parents enjoyed enthusiastic games of hide and seek as though they'd never played it before. They had to set boundaries, so nobody strayed too far away, making it impossible to find them. They also played skipping with two people turning the rope, and others jumping in when they could. Usually, this ended up with participants lying exhausted on the floor, wreathed in smiles. In general, they had to work hard to be self-sufficient, but the chores became easier as they became more proficient and the leather idea worked, providing most of them with new moccasins.

As the years went by, their children ran everywhere and learned from the adults how to live off the land. Phil became known as *Mr Fixit*. He could work on almost anything, so it was a well-justified title. He mended the lawn mower, and he and Jose cut the grass at the front of the house. Between them, they put up makeshift fencing around the perimeter to reinstate the tennis court which once stood there. They mended the old nets, rummaged in the attic until they found racquets, which only needed a few running repairs, and among all the junk kept in the attic, they found a box of new tennis balls. Soon tennis matches were being organised and there were regular competitions. The older ones could only marvel at the energy levels displayed by the young even after working on their chores all day.

To be so self-sufficiently happy with their lives on the farm after the horrors of the plague years was a wholly unexpected boon for the adults and privately they all prayed the hard times were gone for good.

36

Annie cried out as she woke from her sleep and Mary was quickly by her side. "Where has everyone gone? Where are all the children?" Who is taking care of the little ones?" Her distress was painful to see.

"Hush now, everything's going to be alright," soothed Mary. "Would you like me to help you take a walk around to stretch your legs?"

Annie didn't answer but looked up into the eyes of this strangely familiar young woman and put her arms up to enable Mary to help her up. Cautiously, Mary got Annie onto her feet and guided her carefully across the farmyard. Annie looked at the farmhouse, but couldn't place it in her memories.

Mary took her to the toilet and helped her wash and refresh herself. That was enough to tire Annie out again. The fever had seemed to be gone but Annie was beginning to shake as though very cold. Mary covered her once more again with the sheepskin, and administered another sleeping draft. Annie soon drifted off.

This time, she dreamed of the children here at the farm. They must have been about three or four years old or perhaps a little older. Two men came to the forefront of her thoughts, and somehow she knew their names to be Jose and Philip but had no awareness of how she knew this to be so.

It was the two men who found the pump. They'd been rummaging about in the barns with a few of the children in tow when one of them – it was Josh; Annie suddenly came through the mist in her thoughts as she remembered Josh was one of the children – Josh tripped over something. He was crying and Jose went to see to him. The poor child had cut his knee and Jose consoled him while Philip investigated what the lad had fallen over. It was almost buried, but he knew instantly that it was of interest.

"Let's get these children back to the others and we can return and dig this up." Josh had stopped crying, but his knee was still bleeding profusely, so Jose agreed. He hoisted the lad into his arms and the little troupe returned to the farmyard to hand the children over to the tender care of the mothers.

The two men returned to their find and excavated the object which they triumphantly carried back and placed on a table for proper examination. The question was whether they'd be able to make it work again. They attacked it with sandpaper and tools and with considerable effort managed to dismantle it. They laid the whole thing out like a jigsaw puzzle, every metal part, every nut, bolt and screw. When they saw it in pieces, Eric and Paddy burst out laughing because they thought the lads would never get all the pieces back together again. How wrong they were. Jose and Phil carefully cleaned off all the rust, greased it all and put it back together. Jose was telling everyone who came to look at what they were doing that Philip wasn't called *Mr Fixit* for nothing. The pair of them then went around every farm outbuilding and asked everyone they met on the route if they had seen any long sections of pipe lying around.

Jim remembered seeing some plastic piping at the roadside, just before they arrived at the farm. "I don't suppose it'll be any good now, after all this time," Jim said to Phil and Jose. Liam said, "I can remember it though. Would plastic perish, do you think?"

"Only one way to find out," said Phil.

"Good idea!" agreed Jose. "Let's go explore."

The four of them were very excited about the coming adventure and set off early the next morning with packed lunches but didn't return at all that day. Some of the group were contemplating forming a search party when the four of them rolled up. They were cheerfully singing "Hey Ho!" like the seven dwarfs from Snow White as they walked in line, shouldering a long, unbent length of pipe from some abandoned highway project.

Immediately they were bombarded with questions. Phil told everyone that he was sorry if they'd been worried, but it turned out to be much further than Jim and Liam had remembered and it was almost dark before they found it. Others were asking what it was like out there and if it would be possible to leave the farm and go back to their homes again. "Did they meet anyone?" was the commonest of the questions asked.

"Slow down," said Jim. "We need food and something to drink. I'm starving."

Everyone gathered around the table as the four of them ate their fill. They answered questions as they sat, but there were no hard and fast conclusions to be had. Then they carried the pipe to the side of the well and left it there to tackle Phil's brilliant idea when they were fresh.

The next day, it was with great pride that the four men presented the group with a fully functioning pump sucking water up from the depths instead of anyone having to dip and raise the heavy old bucket. Even the smallest child would be able to work it. They all stood around while the pump was used by anyone who cared to try it and, each time a container was effortlessly filled with fresh water, a cheer went up.

A few days later, Jim, who had, over time, become the unchallenged leader of their community, asked all the adults to meet in the farmhouse for an important discussion. Angela suggested the meeting could be combined with their main meal, as everyone would be available then and she'd ask Margaret to broach some of her elderberry wine which test-sampling had shown was definitely ready to drink. It was agreed that the meeting should take place in the evening.

After they'd eaten, Jim called for their attention. "As you know," he began, "we four ventured outside for that pipe and we've been wondering if we should have a look further afield to see what's occurring out there. Do we have any volunteers?"

They all started to talk at once to whoever was next to them. Jim tapped on his glass. They all stopped talking and looked to him for guidance. "One at a time," he said.

Mike said, "Why don't we all go?"

Martin agreed. "We need to know if things are getting back to normal out there."

Alex said, "Until we go back out there, we'll never know if the pandemic has ended, and I for one never intended to become a farmer. Not that I haven't enjoyed it, but it would be good if we could watch a television programme again..." He trailed off, not wishing the others to think he was out of order.

The buzz of voices started again.

Jim tapped his glass again. "Can I just go around the table to each of you for a yes or no on that question?"

There were nods of agreement.

He went round the table, starting with his wife Rosie, sitting on his left. The answer was yes in every case until he came to the older group members, Annie, Eric, Paddy, Sharon, Angela, Ralph and Barbara. They all said no, on the grounds that they weren't fit enough to go traipsing about the country or fast enough to keep up with the rest of them.

Then Sharon asked, "Wouldn't it be a good idea to leave the children here with us on the same grounds? And it would keep them away from any danger out there."

Rebecca asked, "Would you be able to cope with so many little ones?"

"Of course we can!" said Angela and Sharon in near unison.

Paddy added, "You won't be gone forever will you?"

"What about taking a vote?" Eric said.

There were no dissenting voices.

"That's settled then," said Jim. "I call this meeting to an end." Not that that stopped further excited discussion about planning the coming adventure and the babble of voices continued well into the night.

The next day, the adventurers prepared the gear they thought they'd need for venturing out into the unknown. They collected containers to carry water and *the oldies* spent hours cooking and packing food for them. There was no telling whether and when they could get hold of further supplies, so it was agreed that they must carry enough for at least two weeks.

Eric told them they could use his car. "I don't think that we used up all the fuel and it will get you further, quicker, and it's easier than walking. You can always dump it if it becomes a burden."

"Good idea," said Jose, "Phil and I will give it a once over. You are quite right, Eric, we would be better off with transport especially if we take the trailer too."

"Come on then, what are we waiting for," said Phil.

They soon had the car up and running. The tyres were not looking too good but Phil reckoned they would be safe enough for the journey. "We don't need to pass an MOT, do we?"

The departure gave rise to lots of tears, hugs and kisses as parents said goodbye to their offspring. It was so difficult because they were all aware what dangers might be lurking away from the relative comfort and security of the farm. Rebecca made Annie and Eric promise to look after Thomas. She was looking through eyes filled with unshed tears. Eric hugged her again. "Of course, we'll look after him."

"I need a promise, Granddad, I know you never break a promise."

Eric coughed to clear his throat. "I promise. But you're only going to be away for a couple of weeks. Three at the most."

Rebecca hugged Thomas again before she put him in Annie's arms and turned away.

When they were all aboard the car and trailer Frank drove slowly away up the hill. Jim and Liam replaced the gate covered in foliage to disguise the track and walked behind the vehicle for a while swishing brushwood to obscure the tyre-tracks. Then they were gone.

37

Mary again came with a potion to help Annie back to sleep. She still appeared to be in a lot of pain. This time, she had Lois and Emma with her.

"Will she be alright?" asked Emma, and Annie was vaguely aware of the girls standing over her before she drifted back into sleep. Mary put her arms around the other two girls and shook her head. "I think she may be dying," she whispered.

Annie was dreaming of the anxious time they'd spent caring for twelve small children and worried sick about the others, hoping all the time that this would be the day they returned but it didn't happen. Two weeks went by, three weeks, and then four. Ten weeks passed with no sign of them. Eric, Ralph and Paddy climbed to the top of the hill most days to see if anyone was in sight but each time they came back down, disheartened.

Sharon was the first one to broach the possibility of them not returning at all. "We just have to carry on regardless," she said, ever the optimist.

"How're we going to manage without them?" Annie asked.

"Same as we did before," Barbara said with determination. Unfortunately, she now spent a lot of her time asleep in Wendy's rocking chair by the Aga. She liked to sit with Mary on her knee telling her all about looking after the sick. Mary, although so very young, appeared to lap up everything Barbara told her.

They carried on.

Young Thomas was a leader right from the start. The other children all followed his example. Sometimes this got them into scrapes, but their confidence in him only grew with time. He knew from his Great-Grandad which berries and mushrooms were poisonous and how to tackle most survival tasks, knowledge he shared with the others. He could milk a cow and thresh the wheat and do pretty much everything necessary around the farm. The one thing which scared him and he left to Mike's son was tending the bees. Craig was such a small boy but very confident that he knew exactly how to look after them without getting stung. He looked cute in cut-down netting and a hat and although Eric used to go with him early on, it soon became apparent that Craig needed neither help nor support and could manage the job easily alone.

The boys and girls ended up all able to drive the tractor although they needed the help of an adult to change the equipment from plough to harrow as the equipment was too heavy for them. Annie and Eric wondered what would happen when they ran out of fuel for the tractors but watching the children working gave them all the courage they needed to go on. Sam had left them plenty of meat, filling the freezer to the brim, and the wind turbines gave them their electricity. Their food would eventually run out but they knew if they ignored the problem they'd have to think of alternative ways to feed themselves.

They sat out around the tables in the farmyard at night and the children asked to be told stories. Adam piped up, "Tell us about Dad. What was he like, when he was little?" Angela and Ralph thought for a while and then started to tell the children about the time when Phil decided to do an experiment using gunpowder he'd carefully scraped from matches into tin foil. Every such story took a long time because it needed to be peppered with explanations of all the things the children had never seen or experienced which *the oldies* had taken for granted for most of their lives. "Phil placed a metal dart into the powder so when he lit it the powder exploding would send the dart flying out. He didn't have the faintest idea the explosion would be strong enough to send the dart straight through Grandma's kitchen door." The children seemed enthralled by such tales even though most of the time they probably had no real idea what the adults were telling them.

119

Somehow the promises made to the missing parents were fulfilled and the children were raised to the best of *the oldies'* abilities.

38

The food from the freezer had long since run out. They killed chickens as and when necessary and Eric and Paddy grew as much as possible in the greenhouses. Some of the children helped them and learnt quickly which plants were weeds, and which were not.

Paddy and Ralph were just coming back from the river, where they had been fishing as they did every day, when two of the children, Adam and Lois, came running up shouting to them to come quickly. They ran into the forest and disappeared from sight. Over the years, a tangled mass of undergrowth had grown up all around the area. Paddy and Ralph had never ventured this far from the farm before but then they heard a sobbing scream. Lois came back to take hold of Ralph's hand and lead them towards the sounds of distress. In a clearing, a man was lying on the ground, Adam kneeling helplessly beside him. When he saw them, the man began shouting in a language neither Paddy nor Ralph understood.

Paddy said, "I think that's Arabic."

"Wherever he comes from, he needs help," said Ralph. They could see the man had badly broken his leg and the pain it was causing him clearly justified his screams. "We'll have to put a splint on it before we can move him."

"Any idea how we do that?" asked Paddy.

They found some branches to place either side of the leg and Ralph surrendered his shirt to be tied around them, encasing the leg, as best they could. While they were doing that, Adam and Lois gathered some longer branches and some vine. It needed cutting, but no one had a knife with them. The injured man tried to shift himself over on the ground and when they saw the handle of a machete trapped beneath him, Ralph helped him to move off it so Adam could grab the massive knife. He used it to cut the vines and tie them over and over the branches, forming a makeshift stretcher which Paddy reinforced with torn strips of his own shirt. They didn't have the strength to carry the man on the stretcher but contrived to pull it along the ground, which worked alright through the long grass until they encountered rougher terrain. Their loud shouts for help attracted Eric and Angela and between them they reached the farmhouse where Barbara took charge. She was the only one of them with any medical skills and even though now crippled with arthritis, she bent over the man on the stretcher to examine his leg.

"Let's get him onto one of the tables so I can have a better look," she ordered. The man let out another scream as they hoisted him, stretcher and all, onto the kitchen table. She cleaned the wound before making a more professional job of straightening the broken bones and rebinding the leg in a better splint. Gradually, the man's moans petered out and he lay quietly, looking around at everyone staring at him.

Sharon came closer and asked his name. He looked bewildered and obviously couldn't understand them, so she pointed to herself saying her name and then naming each of the others in turn. Before long the man nodded and pointed to himself, saying something which sounded rather like Zack, so from then that's what they called him.

In the attic, Paddy found a set of crutches which old George mentioned having after hip replacement surgery years before. Zack got on famously with them and his leg slowly healed although he would walk with a severe limp for the rest of his life. They never found how he had survived or where he had come from because of the language barrier none of them ever really conquered, but the children adored him. He took them out and showed them how to catch far more fish than Paddy and Ralph had been able to. He also taught them how to catch rabbits in a snare. The girls, as well as the boys, became very adept at it. They all came to acknowledge that without Zack's skills and help life would have been much more difficult.

The family grew so fast, becoming very healthy and vital teenagers. The outdoor life suited them well and none of them developed any kind of serious illness. Zack had been with them five or six years and he'd taught them to build their own shelters. The benches and tables were no longer the focal point in the farmyard and these had fallen apart long ago. This area was now a campfire, around which they all sat cross-legged, chatting about their adventures. *The oldies* took chairs outside on the few occasions when they joined them. The youngsters were very self-sufficient. Cooking and sourcing food no longer rested entirely on their shoulders anymore and roles were gradually reversing as the children began to look after them more and more.

Zack taught Mary and James all he knew about which were the edible flowers and herbs. For instance, the marigolds growing in the garden could have the flowers steeped in boiling water for a while and then when cooled and strained could be dabbed upon dry or cracked skin to give some measure of relief. He showed Angela how to mix lavender florets with apples to give an interesting flavour and that dandelion roots and leaves were edible. The teenagers learned that rubbing dock leaves onto the skin calmed nettle rash. Angela tried cooking the leaves and they were edible but not very palatable, as they tasted bitter. Rose hips were collected and cooked with a little honey because Sharon remembered Margaret giving something similar to Barbara when she was struggling with a heavy cold. Zack indicated that the roots of cowslips and primroses could ease chestiness and Mary tried the remedy out on Ralph when his breathing became shallow. It worked fairly well, although by then he was too ill for it to be anything like a cure. Evening primrose was picked and its bright yellow petals were eaten in salads while the roots had a nutty flavour and the seeds when crushed were turned into oil for use in cooking. Poppy seeds were also crushed and Zack taught Mary and James what to use them for.

Zack demonstrated how to cook in a pit dug in the ground and they parcelled fish in leaves held in place with willow bark strips and cooked it over hot stones covered in soil. A long stick down into the pit was removed, leaving a hole through which water could be poured down onto the hot stones. This caused steam to rise, and after a while, the food parcel was dug out and it proved absolutely delicious.

Not all of the food looked or tasted as delicious and one day, Sharon looked at the offering on her plate and said there was no way she could eat it.

Paddy said, "I'll tell you a story. One day, my Granddaddy went out with his Grandpa. He had stayed overnight and they were up and ready by four am. His Grandma was cutting thick slices of homemade bread, and spreading them with something which looked like lard. Gingerly, he said to his Grandma, *I don't like that*. Quick as a flash she replied, 'You will' and by the end of the long day, he did because he was so hungry. So, Sharon my love, get it down you and be grateful you've something to eat." They all laughed, and ate even if the dish was unlikely to ever become a favourite for any of them.

Eric and Paddy often went down to the river to see what was cooking in the encampments. Unfortunately, Ralph could no longer go out with them. He was getting worse and had suffered constant pain in his chest. His breathing was shallow, and he now spent all his time in bed. Angela was run ragged nursing him and they all knew the end was near, but no one wanted to acknowledge it.

39

The oldies' young charges were no longer reliant on the farm for their survival. They had become quite capable of living off the land. Every one of them could hunt, fish, and make serviceable clothes and footwear, although they mostly ran about bare footed.

Thomas was the one who decided who was best suited to which job. Lois and Liam, the inseparable twins, were responsible for a steady supply of fish from the river. Adam and Susan always joined the hunting party, both being excellent archers, using bows and arrows made under Zack's watchful eye. Craig, of course, looked after the bee hives. James and Mary knew it all about plants and berries and Mary gave Eric an infusion of red clover and violas which helped him when he had a bad cough. They also made sure that when the hunters stayed out in the winter time all night, their faces were covered with goose grease, to help against the cold. The winters were warmer now but still chilly in the depths of the night. Emma, Josh and Megan prepared the rabbits or any other small game, and collected potatoes which now grew wild, keeping everyone well-nourished.

Thomas did a bit of everything, and with the help of Susan, his best friend, made sure things ran smoothly until the day an agitated Craig came running into the farmyard. He was extremely distressed, and could hardly talk because he had run so fast and was breathless. Thomas made him calm down. Craig gasped and gulped a few times and then told them, saying that the bees had swarmed. They didn't understand the significance.

"What does that mean, Craig?"

"It means disaster. It means disaster," yelled Craig.

By now, Eric and Paddy had joined them to see what the upset was about. Eric put his arm on Craig's shoulder. The gesture was enough to calm the lad.

"Sorry but my Dad told me when bees swarm and disappear, it's an omen of bad things to come."

"Can we find where they have gone?"

"I don't know."

Paddy said, "What do you think Tom? Should we go out and try to find them?"

"We could go tomorrow with Craig," agreed Eric.

"Good idea Granddad. I can't spare anyone. We're all going hunting because we're getting short of fresh meat."

Craig calmed down. "Do you think we'll be able to find them?" he asked.

"We can give it a jolly good try," said Paddy cheerfully. They all knew that Craig treasured the fact that his Dad had left the hives in his care, and now they were empty.

The next day, the hunt went well and they caught a deer. Whilst it was being roasted that evening a party atmosphere developed with the drums being beaten and their penny whistles blown excitedly. Then they ate their fill and danced around the campfire until they slumped down exhausted.

Angela didn't join in. She had stayed in the farmhouse to look after Ralph. When it began to get dark, Sharon, Paddy, Eric and Annie went back to find Angela sitting in the rocking chair, by the Aga, with tears flowing down her cheeks. She had no need to tell them Ralph had gone. Sharon put the kettle on, her answer to all sadness. Eric turned as if to go back outside to the youngsters but Angela looked up and said, "Don't spoil their fun. Ralph can stay where he is tonight."

The funeral next day was an emotional affair. Afterwards, Eric and Paddy went off with Craig again to look for his bees and the rest of them went about their work. Survival brooked no real down time.

Paddy and Eric followed Craig up the side of a hill, covered with heather, which they were finding quite hard work to keep up with the young lad. Craig was well in front of them as he was determined to find his precious bees. Paddy said quietly to Eric, "I don't know what he's going to do even if we do find them. I bet he has no idea how to get them back to the hives." Eric had no suggestions for that either.

On that day the twins returned from the river with only a handful of fish in their basket. They went straight to Thomas to show him explaining that the water level in the river was very low. "We only managed to get these few," said Lois. She held out the basket for him to see.

"I told you it was a bad omen when the bees swarm," moaned Craig.

"Keep that to yourself," warned Paddy. "We don't want panic, do we?"

Later Thomas came into the kitchen to talk to *the oldies*. "I think there must be a blockage further upstream. We need to go tomorrow to find out."

Eric and Annie were worried that could be dangerous but Thomas said, "Without the river, we could all be in danger. Without the fish for food, we'd struggle to feed us all." They all knew he was right.

"We'll be back before you know it."

Thomas took Susan, James and Megan with him. They carried leather pouches with water and snares for catching rabbits and small game. Zack had taught them well in the art of survival.

This left the twins, Lois and Liam, Josh, Adam, Mary, Emma, Craig and last, but not least, Chloe, to hold the fort. Zack was less of a help these days, his leg giving him a lot of pain.

That night, Annie cried in Eric's arms until she fell into a fitful sleep. When she was still miserable the next morning, Eric just said, "We have to carry on. Our role in life is just to make sure these precious youngsters survive. Don't you read your bible? They're the meek and they shall inherit our Earth."

Annie shook her head. "We are all getting too old for this."

Eric and Paddy quoted her sister, Barbara, "The cup is half full you know."

"Seriously, though, Barbara would be turning in her grave if she thought we were about to throw in the towel," added Sharon.

By Annie's reckoning, Thomas' group had been gone for at least three months, but Eric was a tower of strength. He would not believe that they would never return.

Craig never did find where his bees had gone, but his consolation came in the form of Emma choosing more and more to be with him, wherever he went.

Then Liam and Lois came back into the camp one day full of excitement and in a great hurry, with more fish than they'd caught in a long time. "The river's getting wider again," they shouted. Liam said, "I also spotted smoke from a fire away in the distance. I bet it's Thomas."

That sparked a celebration and they hoped the wanderers could hear the faint sounds of drums on the evening breeze wherever they were camped.

40

The next day began as usual with Angela settling down after breakfast in her favourite rocking chair, which she had done a lot of since Ralph died. Maybe she was giving up because even her great-grandson, Adam, couldn't keep her cheerful these days.

Today of all days when they were anticipating the return of their travellers, the weather chose to turn cold and it was threatening to rain.

Eric and Paddy had set up a chess game because they weren't going to venture out. Sharon put wood on the Aga and soon they were very cosy in the farmhouse kitchen. Annie was washing the dishes and Sharon had got out the bowls ready to make cakes when it began to rain.

Suddenly, the sky darkened, and in the distance, the first lightning flashed followed by a roll of thunder. The storm came progressively nearer. Eric and Paddy stopped playing to sample Sharon's griddle cakes as she called them because the oven was broken and they'd been cooked on the hob. Cooking was a rarity these days for her and she was pleased with herself for making the effort. "If you'd like to take these over to the huts for the children Annie, I'll clear up and we can eat ours with a nice cup of nettle tea."

"Will do," Annie said. "The rain seems to have slowed a bit, so I'll go now."

As quickly as she could Annie headed for the nearest hut in the yard. Inside she found the girls huddled together with fear in their eyes, but before she could utter a word of comfort, there was an almighty flash of lightning followed by the loudest of crashes. The hut shook as the ground rumbled. The returning storm was directly overhead. The girls screamed, and they all ran outside gripped with fear. They found themselves staring at a pile of rubble where the farmhouse had been.

There was nothing anyone could do. The lightning had uprooted the huge cedar tree which had stood proudly by the side of the house since it had been built hundreds of years before and the toppling tree had crushed the house and everyone inside it.

The rain was pounding down as they tried to pull the stones away, but it was no use. Annie could hear someone screaming hysterically until she suddenly realised that the sound was coming from her own lips. "Why didn't I stay in the house?" she screeched.

The boys and girls all began to methodically pass stones away from the building and periodically Josh told everybody to be quiet so he could listen for any sound of life but to no avail. They all had to stop because of exhaustion and bleeding hands. Annie's fingers were bleeding too and she was shaking from cold and weariness.

As suddenly as the storm had begun, it stopped. There was an eerie silence after the beating rain. Annie stood still, unable to move, totally engulfed by the loss of Eric and her lifelong friends. The girls helped her, zombie-like, back inside their hut. She allowed them to take off her sodden clothes and cover her in something warm and dry.

Annie re-emerged into a hot, sunny day but immediately she began to shake uncontrollably again. A young woman helped her to lie down on a bed of sheepskins. She had no idea who the girl was. As she lay there, familiar faces started to come and go in weird shapes and sizes. She saw her precious Eric. He smiled and held out his hand. When she reached out to take it, he disappeared. She lay there on the bed, not realising what had happened. Tears ran down her face, and eventually, she slept.

They say that just before you die, your whole life passes before you in an instant. Annie thought about Sharon, her best friend, and how much fun she'd had with her and Angela during their lives. Then her musing mind settled on Eric and their life together and their children.

The sun was still bright in the blue sky so she guessed that she must have been asleep for at least two hours, unaware it had been two whole days. From nowhere, a cloud passed over the sun, and she shuddered. Almost immediately the sun glinted in her eyes again, and she could see the silhouette of a man. "Is that you Eric?" she croaked.

"No Gran, I'm Thomas." He leaned over Annie and placed a new-born baby into her shaking arms. "This is my son, Eric," he said, gently. Annie smiled. The baby opened his eyes which were a piercing blue and looking straight at her. She gently stroked his soft cheek as he reached up to clutch her finger.

As Annie closed her eyes for the final time, she saw Eric standing there smiling. Sharon and Paddy were there too, and, alongside them, Angela and Ralph. They were holding out their arms and beckoning her to join them. Her life had at last gone full circle.

EPILOGUE

Thomas decided that they should begin the journey back along the river to a place where they had found caves. He argued that they would be better able to survive there given that the farm and surrounding area had been so completely devastated by the storm. His companions looked around them and in turn nodded in agreement.

They did survive and perhaps it was their drawings and tools which were discovered centuries later in the caves at Creswell Crags.

They weren't alone. Many other small groups around the world also survived. The meek had indeed inherited the Earth.

Millions of years later a huge stone door was unearthed in the middle of a city. Once opened, steps were discovered leading down into the ground...

FICTION FROM APS BOOKS

(www.andrewsparke.com)

Andrew Sparke: *Abuse Cocaine & Soft Furnishings*

Andrew Sparke: *Copper Trance & Motorways*

HR Beasley: *Nothing Left To Hide*

Jean Harvey: *Pandemic*

Lee Benson: *So You Want To Own An Art Gallery*

Lee Benson: *Where's Your Art gallery Now?*

Michel Henri: *Mister Penny Whistle*

Michel Henri: *The Death Of The Duchess Of Grasmere*

Nargis Darby: *A Different Shade Of Love*

APS PUBLICATIONS

29837977R00074

Printed in Great Britain
by Amazon